CW00550753

THE
LODGER

JOANNE RYAN

ISBN: 9798405944166

Tamarillas Press

Cover Design: © Joanne Ryan

Other books by Joanne Ryan
One Night
Lie to Me
The Double
Without Reason
All the Lost Years
Not Your Average Girl

Writing as Marina Johnson
Fat Girl Slim
Fat Girl Slim Returns
Fat Girl Slim Three
The Harriet Way
The Herb Sisters
Say Hello and Wave Goodbye
So Talk To Me

CHAPTER ONE

Gina

L issa moved in to the house next door to me the year I turned twelve. It was the first week of the school summer holidays and I watched from my bedroom window as the three burly removal men unloaded their furniture and lugged it up the driveway and into the house.

Debbie from number seventeen and her best mate Yvonne were standing at the end of Lissa's driveway and quite brazenly watching. I remember that the two of them never seemed to feel embarrassed or awkward and if they wanted to do something they just did it; no doubt they're still like it now.

How I yearned to be like them.

Eventually, nosiness got the better of me and I summoned up the courage to venture out of my bedroom and go down and stand outside and watch the removal men. My plan had been to stand near to Debbie and Yvonne and pretend that I was with them. When I arrived, they looked at me and sniggered and pointedly moved to the other side of the road so I was left standing awkwardly on my own. I had to remain where I was to save face, even though I wanted to go straight back indoors and run up to my bedroom and hide.

My parents and I lived at the posh end of the street. Lissa's house might have technically been next door to ours but it wasn't actually close to us because the houses and their surrounding gardens were so big. Our house had five bedrooms, far too big for just myself and my parents (if you didn't count the au pair) and had a massive garden and long driveway. This was one of the reasons that Debbie and Yvonne called me a snob because it was quite grand compared to the houses they lived in. I wasn't a snob at all; I was just different to them.

Debbie and Yvonne lived at the other end of the street where the houses were semi-detached and the gardens much smaller; they were built over ten years after ours were built when several of the house owners sold off their huge gardens to developers. I couldn't remember them not being there but my parents weren't happy about the *new* houses as they called them; they thought they lowered the tone of the area and detracted from the value of ours.

Not that they told me any of this; I only knew because I was adept at eavesdropping. I used to stand on the landing at the top of the stairs listening to them when they thought I was in bed. I'd hear the chink of glasses and listen to the gossip because it was the only way that I ever found out anything. So, I wasn't a snob but my parents definitely were.

When I first set eyes on Lissa I was awe-struck; she was beautiful. Lissa was the same age as me but she seemed so much older and more sophisticated. I was gawky and awkward, she was perfect. She had blond, curly hair, big blue eyes and long, lithe limbs; the very opposite of me with my lank, mouse-brown hair and stick-like legs that had no shape at all. I'd had a growth spurt over the previous months and was a good head taller than most of my peers. I thought, at the time, that I was deformed and would never stop growing and would turn into a giantess. It's laughable when I think of it now but then I truly believed that there was something seriously wrong with me. In actual fact, I never grew any taller and I've been the same height since I was twelve and now, I'm not tall at all, just average. But at twelve-years-old I felt like a freak and I hated myself and I just wanted to be like everyone else. I would stoop to try to make myself appear shorter but I made myself stand out even more.

Astonishingly, despite my self-hatred and awkwardness, Lissa and I became friends.

I'd been the odd one out at school for as long as I could remember, despite my inept attempts to fit in, and I expected Lissa to ignore me as most of my classmates did. I hung around with the other *non-populars*; the swotty, too-clever ones and the gormless, un-clever ones and thought that was my lot in life.

So, when Lissa's mother pulled up behind the removal van in a sleek, shiny car, and Lissa climbed out of the car and came straight over and started talking to me, I thought I'd died and gone to heaven. This wonderful creature was actually talking to me as if I were a normal girl instead of an outcast. Debbie and Yvonne had already become bored with watching the removal men and had gone home. I'd lingered because I had nothing else to do and I often wonder if Lissa would have bothered with me if they'd still been there.

Most likely, not.

Lissa, as it turned out, could talk for England, as my mother used to say. But that was fine by me because I was a good listener and I mostly never had much to say for myself. Lissa was funny and also charming, although I wasn't aware of that at the time because I had no idea what charm was. I do now, of course.

Never underestimate the power of charm. I think, if I could choose one gift to have it would be charm because looks fade eventually but charm never does. It seemed unfair to me that Lissa had both while I had neither.

And so began the best summer of my life; and I can honestly say that it's never been bettered in the twenty-one years that have followed. The weather, in my memory at least, was perfect every day and Lissa and I spent the days riding our bikes around in the never-ending sunshine and exploring the town. Lissa had no fear and we cycled miles to places that I'd never been to before even though I'd lived in the town all of my life.

Now when I look back, twelve seems so young; far too young to be cycling off for hours on end or getting the bus into town but it didn't seem that way to me then, it felt quite normal and natural. The more time I spent with Lissa the more my confidence grew; she listened to what I had to say and I didn't feel foolish talking to her. I was overjoyed when she laughed at my feeble jokes and seemed genuinely interested in what I had to say. At last, I thought, I've found a proper friend.

My parents both worked long hours and Maria, the Spanish au pair they're hired to babysit me, didn't care one bit where I was as long as I was back in the house by the time my parents arrived home from work. I think that Maria had her own life whilst I was out of the house but that suited me as long as I could do what I wanted. I knew instinctively, without her telling me, that if I wanted freedom I had to keep my whereabouts a secret and my mouth firmly shut.

Lissa's mother didn't work but she never seemed to be around very much. She was always popping out to the hairdressers or beauty salon or to see friends and never seemed to mind where Lissa went. Lissa had a door key to let herself in and out and I was so jealous; she said her mother trusted her and as long as she was sensible, she didn't mind where she went.

I once overheard my mother refer to Lissa's mother as a *trophy wife* in a sneering tone but at the time, I didn't know what that meant. My mother had a disregard for anyone who didn't work long hours as she did; she thought that being a solicitor was far more important than bringing up her own child. As for my father; he considered my upbringing to be my mother's responsibility. I often wonder whether they ever intended having children or I was a mistake. I asked my mother this when I was older and she said not but as I now know, she was a liar.

The days flew by and I never wanted that summer to come to an end but I knew that it must. When I discovered that Lissa was going to start at the same school that I attended in the September I was overjoyed and secretly hoped that she'd be in the same class as me. I couldn't wait for everyone at school to see that I *was* worth knowing. I knew that my peers would be jealous that someone like Lissa had chosen me as her best friend.

Of course, we weren't in the same class, that would have been too much to hope for, but I consoled myself with the fact that we'd still see each other every day because we lived next door to each other.

Once we'd started the new term, Lissa might have been the new girl and not known anyone but she was soon one of the most popular girls in the school - just as I knew she would be. Everyone wanted to be her friend and she slotted seamlessly into life at her new school. Much more easily than me, even though at first she didn't know anyone except for me. She was pretty and clever and funny and everyone wanted to be with her and *be* just like her. In no time at all Lissa was welcomed into the group of the most popular girls and they'd parade around the school in a cloud of strawberry lip gloss and shiny hair; even making the drab school uniform somehow look glamorous.

I felt proud that she was my friend and I couldn't help preening when everyone could see us as we walked into school together each morning. My stoop had gone and I now walked taller, feeling good that Lissa was happy to have me as a friend.

Each day, as soon as the final bell rang at the end of the day I'd rush out of my classroom and wait outside her form room to meet her so that we could walk home together.

Except that things had changed.

Now that Lissa had other friends she didn't need me anymore; on the third Monday of the school term, I arrived outside her form room at the end of the day and she'd already gone. I told myself that she'd forgotten; kidded myself that I was late and I'd missed her, but deep down, I knew. It was confirmed to me the next morning when I called for her, as I always did, so that we could walk to school together. I can still remember the devastation that I felt when her mother said that she'd already left.

I couldn't believe that Lissa would do that to me; we were best friends.

The next day I set my alarm extra early and got up and got ready for school so I could watch out of my window to make sure she didn't leave before I called for her. I knew she was there but when I called for her and her mother answered the door, she told me that she'd already left. Even if I hadn't been watching and known that there was no way I'd missed Lissa leaving the house, her mother's face told me all I needed to know. She wasn't a good liar. She was friendly and warm, unlike mine, and her face flushed and she wouldn't meet my eyes when she said Lissa had already left.

I knew then that our friendship was over.

I'd been used.

A not uncommon event in childhood friendships and although I was heart-broken at the time I got over it, as children do. There were no more weekends of bike rides and trips to the library or to the park; no more camping out in each other's back gardens or sharing a bag of chips from the chippy. My summer of friendship had been erased and to Lissa it was as if I'd never existed and she avoided me at school until I took the hint and stopped pestering her. I eventually returned to my swotty friends who were only too pleased to welcome me back to the ranks of the outcasts.

The years went by and our lives moved on. We

left school and went to different universities and if we saw each other in the street when we were home for the holidays, we were polite to each other if our paths crossed, but we were never close again. I made no attempt to rekindle our friendship because although I might not have been one of the popular ones, I did have my pride.

She got married – of course I wasn't invited as we were on nodding terms only by then – and once again from the privacy of my bedroom window I witnessed her leaving the house. This time she was in a fairy-tale wedding dress on the arm of her proud father, and I remember thinking how beautiful she looked as they got into the limousine. I'd seen her husband-to-be and he matched her perfectly; handsome, sure of himself, career-driven and from a family wealthier than Lissa's. It was my mother who informed me of his family wealth as somehow, she always seemed to know these things. I was a disappointment to my mother and although she never actually uttered the words, her behaviour towards me made no secret of the fact that I'd let her down by not finding a good prospect to marry. Lissa had married up, as they say, and done very well for herself.

As the years went by, I mostly forgot about our friendship and that one amazing summer, and my life moved on. My parents moved away from the street quite soon after Lissa got married so I had no reason to go back there and our paths never crossed again. We live in a large town and I can truthfully count on one hand the number of people from school that I've bumped into since I left.

After I'd finished university, I began what turned out to be a very successful career in financial services. Once I'd gained experience in a large financial management company I set up on my own and I now have my own successful business. It may sound dull but it's the perfect profession for me because numbers never let you down; they don't cheat or lie and you know exactly where you are with them.

My life is good and although I'm still single, I've had my share of casual boyfriends but no one who I could ever imagine wanting to settle down with.

Until now.

James and I are taking it slowly; I want everything to be right this time. I'm only thirty-three and there's absolutely no reason to rush. I'm hopeful though, because although we've only known each other for a short time he is absolutely perfect. Unbelievably, I can't find one single thing wrong with him and what's more, he seems to think that I'm perfect, too.

So, I'm no longer the sad little girl that I was; I have a house and a successful career and friends too, things that I never thought possible when I was a child. As the years have gone by I've thought of Lissa less and less. When I do remember her, I imagine her living in a perfect house with her perfect husband and most likely, perfect children. I honestly thought that I was unlikely to ever see her again.

Until, one day, she turned up at my door.

CHAPTER TWO

Gina

One of the things about being a financial advisor is that if you're not stupid and you take your own advice, you can set yourself up to be financially secure for life. Pretty obvious when you think about it but believe me, I know plenty of financial advisers who are up to their eyes in debt.

Not me, though.

The advice I always give is to invest in property because you can't go wrong. There are other, faster ways to make more money but they're riskier, too. When you buy property, as long as you're not buying at the peak of the market it's pretty much guaranteed that your investment is going to increase in value. Even if you were to buy at the peak, if you wait long enough it'll most likely come good.

I could have stayed in my flat and bought a buy-to-let property to rent out but several things put me off; the additional stamp duty payable on a buy-to-let, the extra interest that I'd have to pay on a mortgage and the capital gains when I eventually sold it. So instead, I put my small flat up for sale and bought the largest, most expensive house that I could afford – which turned out to be an executive style, four-bedroom detached house with a large garden in a very desirable location. Two of the bedrooms are ensuite, there's a large kitchen/diner and a utility room and an additional formal dining room. It also has the all-important double garage that all up and coming professionals aspire to.

A four-bedroom house with just me rattling around in it does seem rather ridiculous but I have to admit that I have hopes for James and I for the future. But until that happens, I took another piece of my own advice that I regularly dish out to clients.

Get a lodger.

I wasn't keen on doing this because I value my privacy but I talked myself into it because realistically, I wouldn't have to see them very often because they'd have their own ensuite bathroom and I'd throw in one of the other bedrooms as a lounge so that the only room we'd have to share would be the kitchen. I think I could cope with that. It makes complete financial sense for very little inconvenience and if it doesn't work or I get fed up with it, I'll simply ask them to move out.

Ideally, I thought, a lodger to rent Monday to

Friday would be ideal. I know that a lot of people lodge in London from Monday to Friday and although this isn't London, there are a lot people that commute here for work. A season ticket on the train probably costs more than renting my spare room. Monday to Friday would mean that I'd have the house to myself for the weekends but although I'd prefer it, it's not a deal-breaker, just a preference.

I composed an ad for Facebook and made the rent significantly more expensive than any of the other rooms that were being advertised on there in an effort to deter undesirables; I need a professional person like myself. I'm not a snob but if I'm going to be sharing my home with someone then I want it to be with someone decent.

Which is how Lissa arrived at my door.

I knew it was Lissa before she even arrived; that's what Facebook profiles are for and I'd had a very good look at hers. Although she would have had no idea who I was from my Facebook profile as I no longer have the same surname and I'd posted the ad on my business profile. My personal profile is set to private so she wouldn't have been able to glean any information at all from that as we're not friends on Facebook. There is no photograph of me on my business page so there'd also be no possibility that she could recognise me from our childhood friendship all those years ago. Although we lived on the same street until she got married, we had very little to do with each other so I don't flatter myself that she would remember me.

Although I remember her; but that's because she's memorable, I'm not. From her Facebook profile picture I could see that she hasn't changed at all; she still has the lovely blonde hair – although maybe it has a little help from the hairdresser now – and her photograph showed that she's even more beautiful than I remember. So I was extremely surprised to learn that she wanted to rent my room. She married *up,* she comes from a comfortable background where money isn't a problem so what could have possibly happened that would mean she has to rent someone else's spare room? I studied her Facebook page but there wasn't anything in the way of clues except for the fact that she hadn't posted anything at all in recent months.

I would just have to wait until she arrived.

I had lots of other interested people contact me – so many that I took the ad down to stop people messaging me. Perhaps I didn't make the rent as high as I could have but it was an amount I felt happy with. I replied to them all but made sure to give Lissa the first appointment. I was curious and wanted to know how she came to be looking to be someone's lodger, although of course, she may not be forthcoming. There was also a part of me, if I'm honest, that was a little bit pleased that I'd done rather well for myself and she couldn't fail to see that when she arrived.

I made sure that my hair was freshly washed,

my makeup applied carefully and that I was dressed casually but smartly. I may not have her looks but I've made the most of what I've got and what the gym can't fix, good clothes can disguise.

The house was spick and span and looking its best as my regular cleaner had been in the day before. Not that it ever looks anything less than pristine as I'm a very tidy person and can't abide mess. I'd bought a large bouquet of fresh flowers from the florist on the corner and arranged them on the sideboard in the lounge. The house looked stunning and I knew there'd be no problem renting the room out. I'm going to ask for a hefty deposit for my own peace of mind.

When the doorbell rang, I made myself count to ten before I got up from the sofa so that I wouldn't look too eager and then sauntered out into the hall. I took a deep breath and opened the door.

❧ ❧ ❧

We're sitting in the lounge; I'm on one sofa and she's sitting on the other opposite me. We shook hands when she came in and I'm not sure if she recognised me but she looked at me and frowned slightly in a puzzled sort of way. I know that I'm going to have to tell her that I knew her years ago otherwise it'll just look odd.

I'll look odd.

Unusually her Facebook photographs don't lie; she's as beautiful in real life as she is in her pictures but underneath the perfectly applied makeup, I can see the merest hint of dark circles underneath her eyes. She seems almost subdued; not at all the way I remember her. When we were children, she'd light up any room that she walked into and was always the centre of attention.

I open my mouth to speak but she beats me to it.

'Gina?' she asks, hesitantly. 'Do I know you from somewhere? I've been racking my brains to think where I know you from because you look so familiar.'

'Well,' I say, with a rueful smile. 'I actually used to live next door to you in Wetherton Avenue when I was a child.'

'Of course!' Comprehension dawns and she looks slightly shocked and then her face breaks into a smile, the old Lissa back for a moment.

'Georgina!' she says. 'My God, where have all those years gone, it was such a long time ago, wasn't it?'

'It was,' I agree, surprised at the sudden rush of dislike that I felt on hearing her call me by my full name. How I hated that name. The school bullies loved to call me George and say I was a boy because of my flat chest and angular features and the fact that I was taller than all the other girls. I blamed my mother for naming me after her father and I hated her for it. I always refer to myself as Gina now and never tell anyone my full name.

There's an awkward silence and I wonder if she's remembering how she treated me. Her memory can't be so bad that she's forgotten, can it?

'Do you keep in contact with anyone from school?' she asks. 'Or are you like me and you never look back?'

'No, I never see anyone,' I say, shaking my head. 'I probably wouldn't have anything in common with any of them now, anyway.'

'I know what you mean,' Lissa says, laughing. 'I kept in touch with a couple of school friends for a few years but then it fizzled out because none of us really bothered to make the effort. Life moves on, doesn't it?'

'Definitely,' I say, with a smile. 'And I'm nothing like the person I was back then.'

'Nor me,' she says, thoughtfully. 'We're all grown up now, aren't we? We've all done things as children that we wouldn't do as adults.' She has a strange look on her face and I wonder if she's apologising for her behaviour all those years ago. Is this her way of saying sorry? Maybe it is – because she can hardly come right out and say it because that would be just too weird, apologising for something that she did when she was twelve.

I don't answer but I feel suddenly light-hearted; she *is* sorry even though she can't actually say it.

I stand up from the sofa with a smile. 'Why don't I show you around the house so you can see if it's what you're looking for?' I want to show off my house; show her that I've made a success of my life and am no longer the shy misfit from all of those years ago.

'That would be great,' she says, standing up.

She follows behind me as I give her the guided tour of the house. She makes appreciative noises at the size of the rooms and the pristine decor – I paid a professional decorator a lot of money to paint the entire house before I moved in – but I feel that her heart isn't in it and by the time we return to the lounge I'm sure that she doesn't want to take the room.

'So,' I say, as we return to our previous positions on the sofa. 'Would you like the room? I do need an immediate answer I'm afraid because I have a list of other people who want to view it if it's not what you're looking for.'

'It's a big house,' she says, not answering my question. 'Do you live here all on your own, Gina?'

'Yes, I do,' I say. I thought I'd already told her this. She doesn't say anything and looks down at her hands. 'But you know,' I say, as the silence stretches and starts to become embarrassing. 'I do have someone special in my life and I'm sure that in the future it'll become a family home, if you know what I mean.'

Lissa's face lights up and she smiles.

'That's great,' she says. 'I'm so pleased for you, it's a fabulous house.'

I don't know why I said that and I feel suddenly ridiculous. I've only known James for a short while and although secretly I hope that he's the one, why the hell did I say it?

I know why: because I don't want her to think

I'm still a sad, lonely, twelve-year-old, that's why.

'So are you only looking for someone to rent short-term?' she asks.

Aware that I've talked myself into a corner with my stupid statement, I think carefully before I answer.

'I can't give a definite timescale, but I'll probably just want a lodger for a year.'

I want her to go now because I feel foolish; somehow, it feels that the tables have been turned and Lissa is interviewing *me* to see if I'm suitable to share a house with.

'That's perfect,' she says, suddenly. 'I'd like to take the room.'

'Oh,' I say, in surprise. 'Are you sure? Because I will be asking for quite a large deposit before I cancel the other people who want to view it.'

'Yes, I definitely do want it,' she says. 'It's ideal; it's close to where I work and I know the area very well. Sorry to be a bit dithery but I'm still adjusting to life on my own and it's all a bit strange. I don't know whether you've guessed but I'm getting a divorce. I need somewhere to stay until our house is sold and I can buy a new place of my own.'

'Oh, I see,' I say. 'I'm sorry to hear that, it must be a difficult time for you.'

'It is.' She looks down at her lap. 'But it's my choice and I have to look to the future. I keep reminding myself that this time next year it'll all be over and I'll feel like a different person.'

'So where are you staying at the moment?' I ask.

'We're both staying in the house but sleeping in separate rooms.' She grimaces. 'It's not ideal although we're being perfectly civil to each other. It's not helped by the fact that I'm the one who instigated the divorce and Hugh doesn't want to split up. He's refusing to move out. I think that he's hoping that if he stays, I might change my mind.'

'Awkward,' I say.

'Very,' Lissa says. 'That's why I need to move out and let him get used to the idea that there's no going back. We can both move on then.'

A bit like you moved on from me. The thought pops into my head before I can stop it. Lissa hasn't changed at all; in my experience people don't. It's still all about her but that's fine, we don't need to be best friends; she's just going to be my lodger for a while.

'I could move back in with *the parents*, of course,' Lissa says, with a smile. 'But I've a horrible feeling they'll forget I've grown up and treat me like a fourteen-year-old. Mum still keeps my room exactly as it was when I moved out and has begged me to move back in so she can look after me. I don't think I could stand her fussing around me even though she means well.' She laughs and I join in.

'So,' I say, when the laughter subsides. 'When would you like to move in?

CHAPTER THREE

Gina

I stare across the desk at Mrs Heppleton and try my best not to yawn. She's lonely and old, I remind myself, and more to the point, she's a very good client.

She comes into my office every Friday, without fail, to discuss her finances with me. She never used to make an appointment but simply turned up unannounced and expected me to be available. If I had another client with me, she'd leave for an hour and return and wait and repeat this until I was free to see her. I put a stop to this by insisting that we have a weekly appointment so that I'd at least know in advance when she was coming. I don't normally do this for clients because it's absolutely not necessary but Mrs Heppleton is my wealthiest client and it's a small price to pay for her continued custom. There is actually nothing *to* discuss with her regarding her finances; her huge amount of savings are invested safely and securely and earning her a very comfortable income. I reassure her of this every week and once I've done so she relaxes and proceeds to tell me about her cat, her visit to the doctors or the neighbour next door who never gets their dustbin in. I try to sound interested even though she tells me pretty much the same thing every week.

My assistant, Susie, knows the drill by now and brings in a cup of tea with two digestive biscuits five minutes after Mrs Heppleton arrives. I'm not unsympathetic but I have a business to run and I can't be spending hours chatting to clients about nothing; which is why Susie is primed to pop her head round the door after half an hour and remind me that I have a meeting to attend. This usually does the trick and Mrs Heppleton takes the hint and tip-taps her way back down the narrow stairs and out onto the street.

'What do you think, dear?' Mrs Heppleton's voice penetrates my thoughts and I try to remember what she's been talking about. I vaguely recall something about the cat or was it a hospital visit? I'm really not sure.

'Well, it's a difficult one,' I say, hedging my bets.

'That's what I thought, dear.' Mrs Heppleton leans forward. 'Even though I know that Samson will be jealous, I do feel another cat will be a companion for him.'

Ah, it's the cats again.

'I'm sure Samson will get over his jealousy,' I say, with a smile. 'And it would be nice for you to have a new kitten, too.'

Mrs Heppleton smiles and picks her teacup up and sips it even though the tea must be stone cold by now.

'You're right,' she says. 'I shall look into adopting a new kitten the very minute I get home. I always feel better once I've spoken to you, dear. You put everything into perspective.'

She's such a sweet old lady and I suddenly feel deeply sorry for her; she has no relatives except for a grasping nephew who's going to inherit everything when she dies. He visits her just enough to keep in favour – usually her birthday and Christmas – and she's pathetically grateful for the tiniest morsel of attention that he throws her way. I met him for the first time when she came in for an appointment because she brought him with her. He struggled, and failed, to hide his delight and surprise when he discovered exactly how much she was worth. It's all going to be his one day in the not too distant future because Mrs Heppleton is well into her eighties. He even has a copy of the will that Mrs Heppleton's solicitor drew up for her as she said she wanted everything to be open and above board.

Mrs Heppleton was married for over fifty

years before her husband died, but never had any children, or in her own words, was *never blessed*. It seems very sad that good people like her are denied parenthood but parents like mine had no problem at all in producing me. Aware that my mind is wandering yet again I bring myself back to the present with a warm smile to Mrs Heppleton.

'Glad I can help,' I say. 'And it's always so nice to chat with you.'

The door opens and Susie pops her head into my office.

'Your three o'clock conference call starts in five minutes, Gina,' she says.

'Thanks,' I say, as Susie disappears back into her tiny office which also serves as reception.

Mrs Heppleton puts her cup down carefully on the saucer, stands up and takes her coat from the back of the chair.

'I'll let you get on, dear,' she says, as she slips her arms into the sleeves.

'Busy day, today,' I lie. 'And unfortunately, not all of my clients are as nice as you.'

She smiles and slowly walks towards the door, handbag looped over her arm. I feel a moment of sadness as I watch her leave; she'll be going home to an empty house with only a cat and the television for company.

Unlike me.

I now have a lodger because Lissa moved in last weekend.

She arrived at my house on Saturday morning, her car filled to the roof with boxes, suitcases, assorted cushions and bric-a-brac wedged into every nook and cranny. Both of the rooms she's renting are furnished so she has no need to bring any furniture. The bedroom has a bed, chest of drawers, bedside cabinet and a fitted wardrobe and the other bedroom has the sofa I used to have in my flat – which is hardly worn – an occasional table and a television fixed to the wall. I was just thinking that she might possibly fit all of the stuff from her car in there when she informed me that she had another car-load to go back and collect.

As I helped her lug it all up the stairs, I reminded myself that as long as she keeps all of her junk in her rooms it won't be a problem. She can keep her doors shut and if she chooses to live in a mess, that's up to her and is nothing to do with me. I don't have to look at it or live with it so it won't be a problem. I couldn't remember whether she was tidy as a child but it wouldn't matter, I told myself, because apart from cooking meals we're hardly going to see each other.

That was what I thought, anyway.

For the first week I *didn't* see her; I could hear her moving around upstairs and there were numerous bumps and dragging noises which I assumed was her unpacking and settling in. I knew that she'd been in the kitchen when I wasn't there because there were plates and bowls in the dishwasher when I opened it on Sunday. I hadn't been home very much as I'd had a busy weekend out and about with James so Lissa and mine's paths never crossed. I felt relieved when I saw the evidence that she'd been tidying up after herself in the kitchen. This confirmed that I'm not sharing my home with some sort of slob because I don't think that I'd be able to cope with that. This was fortunate because I realised that I should have mentioned this in the advert. I breathed a sigh of relief that Lissa appears to be a tidy person.

I didn't see her all week and aside from the dishwasher filling up more rapidly, I wouldn't have known there was another person living in my house. Whenever I went upstairs her doors were firmly closed with only the murmur of the television giving away the fact that she was in there. What was the normal protocol for lodgers, I wondered, do I knock on the door and ask her if she's settling in okay? I had no idea, never having known anyone who had a lodger, so I did nothing.

I was just starting to feel uncomfortable about the situation and thinking perhaps that I *should* do something when the decision was taken out of my hands. When I arrived home from work last night, I went straight into the lounge and flopped down on the sofa. I'd had a busy day and had spent the afternoon visiting one of my clients who lives out of town. Having driven home in driving rain, in the dark, it was all I could do to kick off my shoes and lay back on the sofa to rest my eyes for a while. I was debating whether to get a takeaway or find something in the freezer to eat when Lissa tapped on the lounge door. I nearly jumped out of my skin because I'd actually forgotten that she was living here. I called out for her to come in and she breezed in and plonked herself down on the sofa and proceeded to tell me all about her week. She said she'd spent all week sorting her stuff out and changing her address on everything and quite honestly, I felt worn out just listening to her. I tried to appear interested but I felt so drained and I was already mentally preparing to bung some soup in the microwave, eat it and then go straight to bed. I think she might have noticed because she asked if I was okay. I told her I was just tired and that it had been a very stressful day and thankfully, she took the hint and jumped up off the sofa and went back upstairs.

But before she went, she suggested that she cook dinner for us tomorrow night.

So tonight, we're eating together.

* * *

As I close the front door the smell of garlic reaches my nostrils; it smells delicious and my mouth begins to water. My stomach growls and it's no wonder; I haven't eaten since this morning and that was only a bowl of porridge. I often skip lunch as I find this a good way to control my weight but the downside is that it results in a sickly headache. I skipped lunch today because I wasn't sure what Lissa would be cooking tonight and if it would be loaded with calories.

'Hi!' Lissa appears in the kitchen doorway, spatula in one hand, glass of wine in the other. She has a pair of checked pink pyjama bottoms on and a fluffy, oversized jumper over the top. Her hair is piled haphazardly on top of her head and fastened with a large chopstick affair through the middle. She should look a mess – I certainly would if I dressed like that – but she doesn't, she looks stunning without any effort at all. I feel immediately frumpy, ugly and fat.

'Hi', I return, pasting a smile on my face. I'm tired and just want to be left alone. I can't be bothered to make small talk over a dinner that I don't want.

'How does Spaghetti Bolognese with home-made garlic bread sound?' Lissa asks.

Before I can answer she continues.

'Oh God, you're not a veggie, are you? I never thought to ask. I should have...'

'It's fine,' I say. 'I'll eat anything.'

'Oh, okay.' She looks a bit surprised and I realise I sound rude and look completely miserable and ungrateful. I'm also implying that no matter how bad her cooking, I'll eat it.

'What I mean is,' I say. 'That I'll eat any

JOANNE RYAN

sort of meat or fish. Spaghetti Bolognese sounds fabulous.'

'Great!' Lissa breaks into a smile. 'I've got wine, too, a nice bottle of red.'

'Even better,' I say, with a grin. I hang my coat up and follow her through to the kitchen. I always shut the kitchen door when I cook so that the smell of cooking doesn't permeate the entire house; I also don't want my coat that's hanging in the hallway to smell of food. I open my mouth to say this and then close it again; that's a conversation for another day, not for now when she's just cooked me a meal. The table is set for two and I watch as she stands at the worktop and pours me a large glass of wine and hands it to me and then tops her own glass up.

'To house sharing!' she says, raising a glass at me.

I raise my glass and we chink glasses. I take a tiny sip and watch as Lissa swallows down a good mouthful. I rarely drink as I like to keep full control of my faculties; I have a very low tolerance for alcohol. But I don't want to look like a party pooper or come across as a tee-total bore so I make myself drink some more of it.

As I sip it, I can't help feeling slightly annoyed at her comment; we are not sharing a house, this is *my* house and she's my lodger.

'Now, sit,' Lissa commands. 'And I'll dish up.'

I pull the chair out and sit down while Lissa fills the plates with food and brings them over. It looks, and smells, delicious.

'Mmm,' I say, twirling meat and spaghetti onto my fork. 'It smells amazing.'

'Well,' she says, with a mouthful of food. 'I don't like to brag but I'm a pretty mean cook.'

I have to agree; spicy and flavoursome, the Bolognese is perfect and the spaghetti is cooked just how I like it.

'So,' Lissa says, between mouthfuls. 'How's your week been – you're in finance, aren't you?'

It sounds incredibly dull when she says it – and I suppose it is, compared to her job. Lissa is an interior designer and works for an upmarket, swish design agency and her job sounds impossibly glamorous; a whirl of visiting rich people in expensive houses.

'Yes,' I say, taking a sip of wine. 'It's very busy at the moment, there's never a shortage of people wanting help to know how best to invest their money.'

'I bet,' says Lissa. 'I may need some help in the future, once the house is sold and the finances are sorted.'

'Of course, glad to help,' I say.

'I'll pay of course,' Lissa adds, in case I think she's expecting a freebie. I feel embarrassed that she felt she had to say it and wish she hadn't. Why is she making me feel as if I'm some money-grabbing financial shark?

'How's the interior design business?' I ask, in an attempt to steer the conversation away from money.

'Busy,' she says, with a laugh. 'And very revealing. Once you're in a person's home most of them reveal far more about their lives than you'd ever believe or they ever intended to. It's almost like I'm a friend rather than a designer. Maybe it's because they're on home ground and their defences are down.'

'Really?' I ask. 'What sort of things do they tell you?'

'Well,' Lissa puts her fork down on the place and picks her wine glass up. 'The one that I visited today is having an affair with her next door neighbour, can you imagine?' She hoots with laughter. 'Her husband has absolutely no idea, the poor sod. Another is planning on kicking her boyfriend out once she's had the lounge done and he's paid for it and another is being stalked! My life is so incredibly dull compared to my clients. Honestly, after a few visits they treat me like I'm their best friend or some sort of therapist.'

I laugh and think of Mrs Heppleton; she's the only one of my clients who confides in me but I can live with that.

'Although,' Lissa adds. 'Some of them *do* become proper friends so it's not always a bad thing. At least I get a chance to get out and about and meet people, I don't think I could stand being cooped up in one place all day with the same people, could you?'

'No, I don't think I could,' I agree.

'And some of the ideas my clients have...' Lissa rolls her eyes.

I raise my eyebrows and Lissa proceeds to tell me about some of the outlandish design ideas that people want. As we chat and eat – although Lissa does most of the talking – I'm reminded what good company she is; funny, self-depreciating and talking to me as if my reaction is the most important thing in the world. The evening flies by and somehow, I seem to have drunk nearly two glasses of wine and invited Lissa to sit in the lounge with me instead of at the kitchen table. This was something that I had no intention of doing as I wanted to keep things strictly landlord and lodger. It doesn't matter, I tell myself, there's nothing wrong with being friends as well, is there?

And then Lissa goes and spoils it all and ruins the entire evening.

'So,' she says, wine glass in hand. 'I kept meaning to ask you, have you been married before? Because you've changed your name, haven't you?'

CHAPTER FOUR

Gina

I have changed my name but I haven't been married before – but that's not what I told Lissa.

I lied and told her that I'd been married briefly in my twenties but it had been a huge, messy mistake and I didn't want to talk about it. She looked a bit shocked and also slightly annoyed, I think, that I didn't want to share the gory details. She said that if I ever wanted to talk just to let her know; she said that as she was going through a divorce herself, we had a lot in common. I didn't say anything but just sipped my wine. There was a bit of an awkward moment and then she started talking again and we chatted and laughed for the rest of the evening.

I think I fooled her; I may have appeared happy and carefree but after she'd commented about my name change, I felt sick inside and couldn't wait for the evening to end.

I shouldn't have lied but she caught me unawares over something that I should have realised she would ask. No one else that I know has ever asked me because they never knew me when I was younger. I should have expected it and been prepared but it's too late now. It doesn't matter that I lied, I tell myself, because she'll never know the truth and when her divorce is finalised and she moves out, I'll know that I'll never see her again.

So why did I lie? There is no great drama behind the lie but I don't want judgement, or worse still, pity, and truthfully, I don't want to talk about it and I have a feeling that if I'd told her she would have made it her mission to find out the story behind it. The reason behind my name change is quite simple; I never see my family and nor do I want to; they let me down repeatedly and I want nothing more to do with them. I don't want their name. I took my maternal grandmother's name of Moray as she was the only one who showed the slightest interest in me when I was growing up; I often wonder how different things might have been if she hadn't died when I was nine. She was widowed and used to look after me while my mother worked and I'd spend the summer holidays at her little terraced house in the centre of town.

How I miss her. Even now.

And now Lissa has asked me and dragged it all up again and made me think about it, which I didn't want to and usually avoid doing very successfully.

My parents don't care about me; they've had no time for me for as long as I can remember and I've always been a nuisance and an annoyance to them. I think I knew that I was done with them the Christmas when I was twelve. My father decided that he could no longer tolerate my behaviour and *washed his hands of me*. It was a while after *the thing we never talk about* happened and I learned of his feelings when I overheard him arguing with my mother. I think I always knew how he felt but to hear him utter the words was a defining moment for me.

I was in my usual listening position at the top of the stairs and they were downstairs in the lounge. I hadn't intended on eavesdropping because I'd been trying to give it up – even though it was the only way that I ever found out what was going on. Giving it up was part of my attempt to turn over a new leaf. To be a better person, to be the sort of daughter that my parents thought I should be.

The decision to be a better person was forced upon me; the threat of being sent away to boarding school was very real and I was doing my utmost to avoid that happening. I knew that I would never be able to cope with living with my classmates for twenty-four-hours a day; I wouldn't be able to hold things together as I could barely manage to do that in familiar surroundings. On some level I knew that if I was sent away then somehow, my behaviour would again spiral out of control and that ultimately, my life would be over before it had even begun. Living at home might not be pleasant but at least I was used to it and could function normally.

I had no intention of eavesdropping that night although I'd actually been doing something that I shouldn't have – rooting around in the spare room. I convinced myself that doing this was okay because I wasn't hurting anyone and more importantly, no one knew I was doing it. I genuinely had no intention or desire to listen in to their nightly argument and even if I'd been tempted, I knew that what I would overhear would in no way be good if it was about me.

I had no fear of being caught eavesdropping or snooping in the spare room because after I'd gone to bed my parents never ventured out of the lounge until they too, retired for the night. This was never before midnight and often much later, by which time I would be sound asleep and they would have no idea what I'd been doing.

The spare room was where Maria, the au pair, used to sleep. It was a nice room with its own ensuite and I'd been trying to persuade my mother to let me move into it. The room was bigger than my own and looked out over our huge back garden. The back garden was green and surrounded by large trees and I could pretend to myself that I lived in the middle of a peaceful forest. My own bedroom looked out onto the street and I was already, even at that young age, finding it depressing watching other people going about their lives and seeming to have a much better time of it than I. Try as I might, I couldn't help comparing myself to others and finding myself wanting.

Maria had left suddenly the week before and in her haste to pack had left some of her belongings behind – or as I told myself, she deliberately left them behind for me. In the top drawer of the chest of drawers she'd left a pink satin bag of makeup holding a half-empty tube of sticky foundation, a black mascara, two scarlet lipsticks and a compact of translucent powder. She'd also left behind a grubby white, padded bra which seemed impossibly glamorous and grown up to me and I would try it on over my non-existent breasts. I was desperate to grow a bust and have a bra like the other girls at school and thought that there must surely be something wrong with me to be so flat-chested. Little did I know that in a matter of months my breasts would suddenly sprout, my periods would start and I'd discover a whole new me.

I never saw Maria actually leave; I went to bed one evening and she was there and the next day when I got up, she wasn't. I was upset about it but couldn't let my mother know this because as far as she was concerned, Maria was the *help*. My mother never knew that Maria and I were friends; after Lissa abandoned me, I confided in Maria and found her to be a good listener and spent many a happy hour sitting in her room chatting to her.

I was bereft when she'd gone; after the loss of Lissa as a friend it seemed particularly cruel to lose another friend. I never even had a chance to say goodbye to her. I wondered if my mother had somehow discovered out friendship and sent her away just to hurt me; she couldn't be bothered with me herself but was jealous if others did. I'd witnessed her on many an occasion berating my grandmother for spoiling me and *listening to my nonsense*, as she called it.

I liked to comfort myself by thinking that the makeup and bra were a parting gift from Maria and an attempt to say *sorry* for deserting me. We never had another au pair after her and my mother ignored me whenever I asked her why Maria had gone. I gave up asking after a few attempts because my mother could never be persuaded to tell me anything that she didn't want to.

I would go into Maria's room and take the makeup bag and bra out of the drawer and lock myself in the ensuite. I'd put her bra on and then put my pyjamas on over the top to see what I'd look like and then make my face up and prance around the bathroom pretending I was grown up. I desperately wanted the makeup for myself but I couldn't take it into my own room because my mother routinely searched it and I knew there would be questions asked if she discovered it.

I'd make myself up and imagine that one day I would fit in and be accepted by the popular girls at school. In my daydreams I would arrive at school one day looking sophisticated and glamorous with my perfectly made-up face and straightened hair and be welcomed with open arms by my peers. Realistically, I knew this would never happen – and it never did – because my mother checked my appearance each morning before I left the house. If she'd detected any trace of makeup, I'd have had to wash my face and remove it immediately. I was fed up with being one of the undesirable, unpopular ones even at twelve-years-old. I was in the group of swotty, studious types but felt that I didn't fit in with them. Yes, I was clever, but I wasn't like them, I was better than them and should have been with the popular ones because Lissa had been my best friend for a while and didn't that prove that I was as good as them?

Anyway, there I was, crossing the landing on the way back to my bedroom when I heard my name spoken from downstairs. There is something about your own name being spoken that makes it impossible not to hear when someone is talking about you and in this case, my father was speaking loudly, almost shouting.

It was after ten o'clock by this time so I knew that they would both be several glasses in to the usual two bottles of wine that they drank every evening. The more wine they drank, the looser and more vicious their tongues became – this is another reason why I rarely drink now. I have no wish at all to be like them. My father was blaming my mother for my behaviour and recent events

– *the thing we never talk about* – and telling her that if she'd been a proper mother it would never have happened. I felt happy when I heard him say this because it seemed as if he was defending me. I agreed totally with him; I have my faults but you can't beat your upbringing, can you? My mother was to blame and I was pleased to hear him confirm this. My mother then began to gabble; the usual self-pitying, self-justifying rubbish that I had heard a million times before about how difficult I was and how she had tried her best and that he was no help at all. This was also true; my father had always been a distant figure and the only time that he ever spoke to me was to admonish me or tell me that I had to *buckle down* and *fit in*.

How I longed to *fit in*; I just needed someone to tell me how.

This was when I heard my father shout at her that he'd had enough and that he could no longer tolerate me or my behaviour and that he was washing his hands of me. I wasn't entirely sure what this meant but I had an idea. I heard my mother laugh bitterly and shout that he'd done that since the day I was born so who would even notice the difference?

Their voices then became even louder and I knew that they would continue shouting for as long as the wine lasted. I remember thinking as I did so that their screaming rows could have been the reason Maria left; unless she was deaf there was no way she wouldn't have heard them because my parents made no attempt to be quiet. I couldn't understand why I hadn't thought of it before.

There were also occasions when my mother would appear with unexplained bruises on her arms and wrists which she would try to hide with long sleeved blouses. Once, she appeared at breakfast with a black eye; she never went to work that day and I'd never known that to happen before. At first, I would ask her where the bruises came from but she would simply stare at me without speaking until she made me feel so uncomfortable that I had to look away. Surely Maria must have noticed the bruises, too?

When I'd heard enough, I quietly went into my bedroom and closed the door. But even with the door shut I could still hear their voices – or perhaps it was my imagination – so I pulled my fleecy dressing gown from the hook on the back of the door and wrapped it turban-style around my head and climbed into bed. I pulled the quilt up over my head and nestled into my cocoon until the morning.

So, there it is. That's the real reason I have a different name to the one I was born with and quite honestly, who wouldn't want to change their name with parents like that?

CHAPTER FIVE

Gina

Already, I'm regretting having a lodger.

I've lived on my own for so long that I've forgotten what it's like to live with someone else. Lissa hasn't been horrible to me or done anything wrong – in fact quite the opposite; she's been extremely nice to me and seems to want to involve me in her life.

She wants us to be friends.

She hasn't said the actual words but her intentions are obvious. She is always pleased to see me and if I'm around when she comes downstairs or we bump into each other she always wants to chat. She says that after the last few months of living in an uncomfortable atmosphere with her husband while her marriage was breaking up, it's wonderful to be able to relax again.

I should be over the moon that she wants to be my friend, shouldn't I? Because didn't I once long for her friendship?

Yes, I did, but that was when I was twelve-years-old and I'm a very different person now. I don't need other's approval and I'm beginning to realise that I don't want Lissa to have any expectations of friendship because I'm not sure that I want to be her friend.

It sounds rather harsh, I know, but the more I get to know her, the less I think of her. It's not that she's not likable and fun, she is. She still brightens up any room that she walks into and she's funny and charming and easy to talk to which are the very reasons that I once yearned to be her friend.

And yet.

Her treatment of me all of those years ago still rankles even though it was so long ago that I should be over it. The trouble is that I'm seeing her through the eyes of an adult now and although she's beautiful and charming and good company, is she a good person?

I'm not so sure.

She confided in me last night that she's *seeing someone*. There's absolutely nothing wrong with that, is there? It's just that I had the distinct feeling that she had her eye on this *someone* while she was still with her husband and that doesn't sit right with me. Perhaps I'm hideously old-fashioned but I don't think that cheating is ever right, no matter the circumstances.

Or maybe that's just the sort of person she is.

A user.

Because when I think about it, she used me. Okay, we were only children but it doesn't make any difference, she used me for the summer so she'd have someone to hang out with and as soon as we started school, she dropped me like a stone without any thought for my feelings. She didn't see me as a friend, I was just someone who was useful for a short while and when I'd outlived my usefulness I was dispensed with.

She's also extremely vain and is constantly expecting to be told how beautiful and wonderful she is. She's incapable of passing a mirror without looking at herself. I've come to the conclusion that she's a very shallow person because everything is about how people look and how much money they have and who has the best job.

Of course, I didn't let her know that I was thinking any of this when she was telling me about this *someone*. I made the appropriate noises and said he sounded lovely and how happy I was for her because that's what was expected of me. And he did sound quite a catch. Although strangely enough she didn't go into detail so obviously her private life is only shared up to a point whereas when she's telling me everyone else's business I get all of the details that I'm sure they wouldn't want shared. Apparently, this mysterious man is drop-dead gorgeous and even richer than her ex (very important to her, she admitted, as she has very expensive tastes and likes to live well) with a huge house that is completely fabulous and to her

49

taste – not surprising as she designed the interior – which is how she met him. It was love at first sight for him and he's practically begging her to move in with him.

I don't know if I completely believe her because according to Lissa, every man who claps eyes on her is immediately smitten and falls instantly in love with her. She is beautiful, there's no denying it, but *every* man she meets can't find her irresistible, can they? If it is true that he wants her to move in it occurred to me that it would be a good thing because then I could go back to living on my own. This wasn't a good thought to have when she's only been living here a matter of weeks but there it is; anyway, she says that it's too early for her to make a commitment like that. She's either lying and he's not as infatuated with her as she says he is or if it's true, she doesn't want her soon to be ex-husband to find out what she's been up to.

It seems that every time I turn around, she's there, wanting to chat or share a takeaway or something and it's all too much. I haven't actually been avoiding her but I have worked late at the office when I would normally come home and finish my work in the comfort of my study.

Who am I kidding? I have most definitely been avoiding her.

My secretary, Susie, has started giving me odd looks when I say I'm working late, and I can't blame her. She knows that if I'm busy I'll always take work home with me rather than stay at the office. I always park behind her in the tiny parking area at the back of the building that's included in the office lease because Susie gets in before me. This is never usually a problem as I'm always the first to leave if I'm not already out on business but on quite a few occasions I've had to go out and move my car so she could get hers out.

I could hardly tell her that I'm avoiding my own lodger, could I? Especially as I'd already told her that Lissa and I are old friends and what great fun it's been catching up with her after all this time. I think I'll go to the gym after work tomorrow instead of working late, otherwise Susie is going to wonder what's going on. Although I don't know why I feel I have to worry about what my secretary thinks but there you are, that's the way I am. Susie has been with me for nearly a year and I don't want to upset her because good secretaries are like gold-dust; I shudder when I think of the parade of unsuitable people that I employed before I found her.

Last night I forced myself to stay and worked alone in the office and it was quite creepy and dark and I couldn't concentrate because I kept hearing strange noises. The building is old and creaky at the best of times and once I'd started thinking about it, I couldn't settle so I gave up at eight o'clock and went home. I thought Lissa would be safely out of the way and ensconced in her own rooms by then but as I let myself in the front door, I could see she was in the kitchen cooking dinner.

I could see this because the kitchen door was wide open. Apart from the fact that this meant I couldn't sneak into my lounge without her seeing me, it also meant that the whole ground floor would stink of whatever she was cooking. I always shut the door when I cook and I have hinted that she should but she obviously doesn't think she has to do what I ask.

She must have heard me come in even though I tried to be quiet because she came straight out into the hallway and started chatting. She then insisted that I join her for dinner as she'd cooked far too much for one person.

What could I say?

I really didn't want to; I like my own company and yet again, I realised that I should never have made the decision to have a lodger. When I imagined someone else living in my house, I thought that I'd rarely see them and that we'd be on nodding terms only if we happened to bump into each other. I now can't relax in my own home because she's always popping up and asking me to have dinner with her or wanting my opinion on a new outfit or her hair and short of being rude, I don't know how to put a stop to it.

When she offered me dinner, at first I said no thanks, I was tired and was just going to heat myself up a bowl of soup and have an early night. Instead of accepting my excuse as I would have done, she looked at me as if I was quite mad.

'Early night?' she demanded, with a smirk and a

puzzled expression. 'At half-past eight?'

I felt ridiculous when she said it. I felt exactly how I used to feel when I was twelve-years-old and at school; the odd one out who didn't fit in, the girl who never knew how to behave and was guaranteed to always say the wrong thing.

I felt stupid.

I forced myself to laugh and say that she was right, maybe half-past-eight was a tad early and that sharing her dinner sounded like a great idea. I then had to force myself to eat a humungous portion of fried chicken and potatoes which I didn't want. Which means I'll have to starve for several days otherwise I'll start putting weight on and it'll be a slippery slope to fatness. Unlike Lissa, I have to watch what I eat very carefully otherwise I'll end up like an elephant, whereas she seems able to shove whatever she likes into her mouth without putting on so much as an ounce.

I had to sit opposite her and talk to her and make conversation when I really couldn't be bothered and try and think of something interesting to say. Although, actually, she does most of the talking so after I'd got a few sentences out she took over so she could talk about herself again. I had to hear all about her fantastic job *again* and how many fabulous friends she has who all love her to bits and truthfully, I wanted to scream at her to SHUT UP.

She even tried to tell me how to furnish and decorate my house. She said she could come up with some great ideas to inject life and colour into my lounge *that wouldn't cost too much* and *would only involve changing a few key items* of furniture. She wouldn't charge for her advice, obviously, she added, when she saw the look on my face. She mistook my annoyance for not wanting to pay but I don't *need* her advice, thank you. I said that I'd think about it but quite honestly, why do I need her to tell me how to furnish and decorate my house? I like it plain and minimal and if there's no colour in it, it's because I *like* it that way. If I want clutter and colour and fancy furniture, I'm perfectly capable of doing it myself. But I couldn't bring myself to say this to her because whereas before she arrived I was perfectly happy with my plain, minimalist house, it now feels as if it's lacking something.

Like me.

Another thing I don't like about her is that she asks far too many questions.

When is James staying over? Do I stay at his place very often? Do I invite my friends around very much? Where does James work? What does he do? Do I still go out with my friends on nights out now that I have James? How are my parents? Where do they live now? Why don't I see James during the week? How long have I had my own business?

On and on and on, question after question.

I felt on the defensive as I do every time she asks me anything and I know it's because I feel inferior to her and feel as if I'm being judged. What I should have said was that we don't all have to jump into bed and have sex with a man the first time we go out on a date with them and that there's no law that says we have to move in together straight away. But I didn't say any of that, I just smiled and told her how James and I met and then wished that I hadn't because I could tell by her reaction that she thought he sounded deadly dull. I obviously can't tell a story like she can because I didn't get across to her how romantic it was when James and I caught each other's eyes across a crowded financial conference. It was fate – not that I told Lissa this – because the conference was over a hundred miles away yet we live in the same town. What are the chances of that? James and I are a meeting of minds and when we decide to move onto the physical stage of our relationship it'll be our business and no one else's.

Certainly not Lissa's.

I evaded the questions that I didn't want to answer and prattled on about trivial stuff until she got bored and wanted to take over the talking again – which wasn't very long because it's all about her. I'm very careful what I say to her because I don't want to have my personal life broadcast to every person that she talks to. She's a gossip; I know all about her clients' personal lives and her workmates lives too. Okay I don't know any of them so maybe it doesn't really matter but that's not the point. I'm sure they wouldn't be happy if they knew she was blabbing their secrets and their sex lives to anyone who'd listen. Also, I'm sure she exaggerates and makes things up to tell a good story.

And I don't like the way I catch her looking at me sometimes; as if I'm still the strange twelve-year-old that she briefly used as a stop-gap until better, more suitable friends came along.

Or maybe I'm imagining it because I'm finding that all of my old insecurities are starting to resurface and I'm feeling unsettled and anxious and that's not good.

So I've decided.

She has to go.

* * *

I didn't go to the gym tonight and I didn't work late either. I came straight home because I'm determined not to be driven from my own home by a lodger. I'd decided that if Lissa appears and suggests dinner or a takeaway – I've never eaten so many takeaways – I'm going to say that I have a headache and don't want anything to eat. Then I'll shut the door of the lounge and put the television on even if she does look at me as if I'm mad.

As it turned out the house was empty when I got in and I quickly hung my coat up in the hallway and then shut myself in the lounge. I'd been home about half-an-hour and was enjoying the peace and lying on the sofa debating whether to cook myself something for dinner or defrost one of the many *Weight Watcher* ready meals from the freezer, when I heard the front door open and close. I braced myself for the inevitable tap on the lounge door and made ready my excuse.

Only she didn't tap on the door, she walked straight into the lounge as if she owned the place and plonked herself down on the sofa opposite me.

'God, what a day,' she said, kicking her shoes off and putting her feet up on the sofa. 'I thought it was never going to end.'

I stared at her, infuriated that she thought she had the right to just walk into my lounge without even knocking. I wouldn't barge into her rooms so why does she think she can treat my rooms as if they're hers? I was going to wait until the weekend to ask her to move out but I decided there and then that I couldn't stand it any longer. I opened my mouth to speak but she beat me to it.

'I was wondering... and you must say no if you don't want me to, but would it be okay if I invite one or two friends over now and then?'

I stared at her. I couldn't tell her she had to move out now, I realised. I'd missed my chance and it would look odd and as if I was saying it because I didn't want her to have friends over. I'd have to wait and ask her later in the week.

'No problem,' I said, generously, while mentally calculating that if I gave her two weeks' notice I'd only have to put up with her for a short while longer. No doubt what she really wants is to invite her mysterious boyfriend over and have him stay the night so she can show him off. No doubt the *inviting friends* over was a precursor to him practically moving in. Although if he has such a fabulous house, why would she bring him here? Why can't she just go to his house and move in with him and leave me alone?

'Great,' she said, settling back on the sofa. I wondered how long she was planning on staying and realised that I might have to use the headache excuse if she didn't leave.

'Fancy a glass of wine?' she asked, with a smile. 'I have a bottle on the go in the kitchen.'

I definitely did not want a glass of wine nor to listen to her bragging about her great life but thought that the moment might be opportune to sow the seed about her moving out so that James could move in.

'Why not?' I answered, despite my previous intentions. I mentally waved goodbye to my peaceful evening.

Lissa jumped up from the sofa, kicking her shoes over in the process and sauntered out to the kitchen. I never wear shoes in my lounge.

I sat back for a moment and closed my eyes and rehearsed what I was going to say to her.

Two weeks, I told myself.

She'll be gone in two weeks.

CHAPTER SIX

Gina

I overslept this morning – I never, ever do this – and I lay the blame squarely at Lissa's door. The glass of wine turned into several glasses and at some point, we ordered another takeaway that I didn't want. Lissa always orders far too much food which she then picks at but for some reason I find myself shovelling down. I've also realised that I'm always the one who ends up paying for it all. Her bank card is always up in her room and it seems churlish to make her go and get it so I pay for it on my card. She promises she'll ping me the money later, but actually, apart from the first time, she never does. I should ask her for her share but I find asking for money embarrassing and vulgar.

I don't even *like* Chinese food very much.

The bottle of wine that she had *on the go,* barely stretched to half a glass each – which was more than enough for me – but she hinted massively that she wanted another glass so I felt that I had to open one of *my* bottles. I don't often buy wine because I rarely drink at home but I do like to keep a few bottles in the house. When I got my bottle out of the wine rack, I noticed that two other bottles that I'd bought were missing so she must have drunk them as I certainly haven't.

As I was in the kitchen uncorking it and fuming that she'd helped herself to my wine (expensive stuff, not the cheap supermarket plonk that she always buys) I resolved to get the *Lissa moving out plan* underway without further delay, which is the reason I drank more than I should have; I needed some Dutch courage.

As it transpired it was a wasted effort because she wasn't really listening because it was all about her, as usual. I told her than I thought James and I were moving to the next level and thinking of moving in together but she never even commented; she was far more interested in telling me how she might be getting a company award for her interior design. The whole night was about her and how wonderful she is and quite honestly, I could have tipped the bottle of wine over her head and gone to bed and left her to it.

I didn't, of course; I sat there politely and said the right things and wished I could go to bed. So I drank far more than I wanted to and went to bed far too late.

Oversleeping wasn't the only reason I was late for work – which shouldn't really matter because

I'm my own boss and can do as I wish – I was also late because I decided that as Lissa is always in *my* rooms, I'd have a look in hers.

I know that it's not on and it's a really bad thing to do but I told myself that it is my house so technically, I should inspect her rooms now and again just to make sure they're okay. And I wasn't actually snooping, just having a look. I didn't rifle through her belongings or anything, I just had a casual look around.

She's not massively untidy; not as neat as I am but then no one is, because I am a bit of a neat-freak. Her rooms weren't a pigsty or anything, there were just a few items of clothing lying on the bedroom chair and a couple of pairs of shoes next to the wardrobe. She'd bothered to make her bed before she left for work which impressed me.

Lissa never overslept this morning despite drinking more than me and going to bed at the same time. She is obviously used to it and can cope with drinking and late nights. I've no doubt she looked fine too, unlike me, I look as if I slept in a hedge and I have a sour taste in my mouth. I felt so rough when I woke up that I thought that I might feel a lot better if I made myself sick but as I hung my head over the toilet, I couldn't bring myself to do it.

As I walked through her rooms it fleetingly crossed my mind that she might have one of those mini cameras hidden somewhere but I dismissed the thought; why would she? She has no reason to mistrust me. Besides, it's my house and I'm perfectly entitled to go in there if I want to.

So I was late for work but that's not the end of the world, is it? Only it felt like it was because the day went from bad to much worse. It was only the fact that Susie had left early for a dentist's appointment that she missed my humiliation at the hands of one of my most important clients.

Theodore Zarkis, all five-feet-six inches of swarthiness and glowering eyebrows, came storming into my office stinking of garlic and aftershave and loudly informed me that he no longer required my services as he had found himself a new financial advisor. An advisor *who does their job properly* he bellowed at me in his nasty way. Theodore is volatile at the best of times and today definitely wasn't the best of times. I could say nothing to placate him. After my first efforts to dissuade him from effectively sacking me were shouted over, I simply sat back mutely in my chair and let him vent his rage at me. Once he had finished, he simply turned around and stomped out of my office with a slamming door as his only *goodbye.* I sat alone and tried to calm myself because his outburst had left me shaken and feeling like the school bully had just beaten me up.

Once I'd calmed down and had a cup of tea, I felt slightly better but still sick at the thought of the commission that I'll no longer earn from him. I will definitely miss the large amount of money that he earned me but I certainly won't miss his foul temper or his misogynistic ways; the man was a pig albeit a very wealthy one.

The situation is entirely my own fault so there's no denying that I have only myself to blame. I was supposed to contact him over two weeks ago to discuss moving one of his financial investments across into a new product but I failed to do so. I tried to explain to him that two weeks makes no difference to the outcome or the amount of profit that he would earn but he wouldn't have it; he said that I had let him down and he could no longer trust me. He's completely overreacting but I'm well aware that other financial advisors are constantly circling like vultures; they're forever contacting him and offering their services so no doubt they've exaggerated the effects of my mistake.

I'm not sure quite how my oversight occurred; Susie is very efficient at bringing important items to my notice every day to ensure that I don't miss anything important. I recall that she has spoken to me several times about Theodore's portfolio so I'm not quite sure how I can have let it slide. The commission from Theodore's portfolio of investments constitutes a very large part of my income and I will sorely miss it. If it had been one of my lesser clients it wouldn't be such a blow but I'll struggle to find another client as lucrative as Theodore.

Especially once word gets out; which it will because Theodore is a spiteful man as well as being an unpleasant one and he'll make it his mission to bad-mouth me.

So, yes, it's entirely my own fault.

But even as the logical part of my brain tells me that, the other, illogical part, shouts out that the real blame lies elsewhere because I've been distracted and made anxious by my lodger. It's all down to the disruption she's caused because nothing like this has ever happened before.

Yes, I decide, irrationally, Lissa is to blame.

It's all her fault.

✻ ✻ ✻

I left work early; after Theodore had stormed out of the office I couldn't settle to anything. I gave in and tidied my already tidy desk at four-thirty and decided to give up for the day and head to the gym. I couldn't face the thought of going home and seeing Lissa and having to make polite conversation with her or God forbid, eat and pay for yet another takeaway that I didn't want. A session at the gym would do me good and go some way towards working off the excesses of the night before.

The traffic is horrendous and it takes me a full hour to get across town to the gym and for a moment I regret not going home; all I really want to do is stuff my face with comfort food and stretch out in front of the television. In other words, have a good old wallow.

But I can't do that because of Lissa; because of her I can't even sit in my own lounge for fear of her bursting in with her dirty shoes and big mouth.

She has to go – and as soon as possible.

I pull up in the car park and turn the engine off and sit in the car and think things through. I'll have a good session on the weights and see if there's a boxing class; I'll feel immeasurably better if I imagine Theodore's face in front of me as I throw punches. An hour here will do me far more good than eating a load of rubbish food that I'm just going to feel disgusted and guilty about afterwards.

As I open the door to get out of the car, a familiar figure in the distance attracts my attention. My heart lifts; James is climbing out of his car which is parked near to the entrance of the gym. Like me, he never usually goes to the gym on a Thursday, he goes on the same nights as me so that we can work out together.

It's fate, I decide; he's been sent by the gods to cheer me up after my dreadful day. Not that I'll ever tell him about Theodore Zharkis; some things don't need to be shared and the less air-time Theodore Zharkis is given, the less it will bother me. I don't see the point in talking everything to death in order to feel better about it.

I hurry myself getting out of the car and I open the back door and retrieve my gym bag from the back seat. If I'm quick getting across the car park, we can go into the gym together. I'm halfway across the car park when I spot her and my heart sinks; Lissa is standing outside the entrance doors to the gym. I'd recognise that jaunty pony-tail and perfect figure anywhere – although she'd be impossible to miss in her eye-popping cerise pink leggings and matching top. Only she could make taking exercise all about what she's wearing.

I slow my pace slightly; I have no wish to speak to her and I curse the fact that she's here. I had no idea that she was a member of this gym. I've never seen her here before although unless she chose to visit at the same time as me, I'd be unlikely to. It's a very large gym and there are so many different classes that we could easily both be here at the same time and not see one another.

I watch as she raises her hand in a wave and smiles broadly. Damn, she's spotted me. I don't wave back but slow my journey across the car park. I know that I'll look rude to her but I don't care; I'm gutted that she's here and I'm going to have to talk to her and possibly even work out in the same area as her. She'll also want to be introduced to James and I can't bear the thought of her speaking to him.

But most of all, despite the fact that I'm ignoring her, I hate that even as I'm walking, I'm making excuses in my head for my behaviour at not waving back at her; I can pretend to her that I never saw her.

I'm disgusted with myself for caring so much what she thinks of me.

Which is when I realise; she isn't waving to me

at all.

She's waving at James.

I see him return her wave and he's smiling broadly, too, and I watch as he joins her outside the entrance doors. I slow to a halt and stare in disbelief as he loops his arm around her tiny waist and pulls her close to him and gazes down at her. She links her arms around his neck and turns her face upwards to him.

I know exactly what is going to happen and I have no way of stopping myself from seeing it. With a feeling of dread, I watch as James lowers his head and kisses her tenderly. I put my hand onto the bonnet of the nearest car to steady myself and lower myself down behind it on shaking legs that have turned to jelly; I couldn't bear for them to see me watching them. After what seems like forever, I manage to raise my head and peer over the bonnet at the gym entrance.

They've gone; no doubt they're going to work out together as James and I always do.

My head starts to pound and bile rises in my mouth and I swallow it down, burning my throat. I take several, deep shuddering breaths and somehow, pull myself upright and stagger back to my car. With shaking hands I manage to open the car door, throw my gym bag onto the passenger seat and collapse into the car.

I cover my face with my hands and wait for the tears to come but my eyes remain stubbornly dry. The tears will come later because at the moment,

I'm in a state of shock and disbelief.

Although as hard as I try, I can't dispute what I saw.

James is cheating on me with Lissa.

CHAPTER SEVEN

Lissa

I couldn't believe it when Georgina opened the door. I realised that I knew her face straight away but it took me a little while to remember exactly who she was. I know so many people and have so many friends that sometimes I totally blank people without even realising it. It's not intentional but I can't remember everyone's name, I'm popular and I know lots of people. I suppose if you only have a small circle of friends and hardly know anyone, you'd remember everyone you'd ever met but that's not me, I'm afraid.

Anyway, by the time we'd got into the lounge it was coming back to me who she was. I'd already pretty much decided that I wanted to take the room – or rather, rooms – because as I walked up the driveway to the house, I could see that the place was absolutely stunning. I was surprised that someone with such a fabulous house was willing to rent out a couple of rooms to a perfect stranger. I certainly wouldn't if it was me. Most of the ads for lodgers are poky flats or terraced houses with barely enough room to swing a cat; and trust me, I know, because I've looked at plenty. It was getting to the point where I was seriously considering moving back to my parents for a while; *that's* how desperate I was.

When I stepped into the hallway it was like walking into a show home because everything was pristine and absolutely perfect. Maybe a little too perfect, if I'm honest; the house is a bit too cold and clinical for my liking but that's the drawback with being an interior designer – I can always see how things can be improved. I knew that I could make my own rooms warm and cosy even though I didn't plan on living here for very long. I was sure that Gina would be only too pleased to have the benefit of my experience for free.

I could have gone home and lived with Mum and Dad – and Mum practically begged me – but I couldn't bring myself to do it.

I'm so delighted that I found Georgina's place because it was seriously getting to the point where I was going to be forced to either go home or rent a place of my own. I didn't want the expense of renting an apartment because I like to live well and not have to scrimp on clothes and going out. What other people see as luxuries are absolute necessities to me and having to watch every penny would drive me mad. Once the house is sold and my money's through, I'll be able to buy a nice house outright and still have funds left over to furnish it nicely and have a comfortable cushion in the bank; one of the benefits of having been married to someone who earns an awful lot of money.

I did lie a tiny bit to Georgina, sorry, Gina, about the reason I wouldn't stay with my parents. It's not, as I told her, because they'll treat me as if I'm a fourteen-year-old (although they would), it's because they're not at all happy that I've left Hugh. They think that we should stay together and *work out our differences*. Daddy went so far as to say that he was rather disappointed in me and that he blamed himself because he thought that they might have spoilt me somewhat. It took Mummy an awfully long time to calm me down after he said that and I cried for so long that my eyes were all puffy – luckily I wasn't going anywhere important that evening – and although Daddy apologised, once it's been said, it can't be un-said. I was extremely hurt that he thought that I was somehow at fault when I'm absolutely not.

Hugh hasn't helped matters by going round to their house and whinging that he still loves me and telling them that he doesn't want a divorce. Honestly, do I have to stay married forever to someone I'm totally bored with? I fell out of love with him a long time ago and I only stayed with him because I knew it would break his heart if I left him. Another reason is that he's reneged on our decision about not having children. When we got together neither of us wanted children and we were both quite emphatic about that. Just because he's changed his mind doesn't mean that I have to change mine, does it? I'm sure if it was the other way around he wouldn't agree to have a baby just because I wanted one. And it's not as if it's *his* body that's going to be ruined by childbirth; he won't be the one giving up his life for the demands of a screaming baby.

But he wouldn't listen to reason and he became a total bore about it and kept trying to persuade me that having a baby would be wonderful and that we ought to do it now before we got too old. He couldn't seem to understand that I don't want a child and I won't be cajoled into having one.

It's his fault that we're splitting up because he kept on and on and on and honestly, he should have a bit of pride and not *beg*. It's just embarrassing.

I could have been really spiteful and made him move out because I'm just as entitled to live in that house as he is but I soon realised that if I didn't leave, he never would. Quite honestly, it's made me lose a bit of respect for him; I'd never lower myself to grovel and beg someone to stay with me

So that's how I ended up sharing a house with Gina. House-sharing isn't quite as bad as I thought it was going to be, it's not exactly fun living with Gina but it's still better than sharing a grotty terraced with loads of other people. After viewing countless house-shares, the only option had been sharing a grubby house with a load of single party-types whereas the reality has been very different. When I realised that I knew her from twenty-odd-years ago, I thought, what are the chances of that? I remembered her, of course, not because she's memorable but because she was a bit strange. I don't mean to be unkind but she was, you know the type, *swotty, spotty and grotty* as our gang used to call them. Not that we said that to their faces, obviously, because we may have been the most popular girls in the school but we weren't bitchy. Well, maybe we were, a bit, sometimes, but that's life, isn't it? You have to use what talents you've been given; you can't spend your life going around like a shrinking violet otherwise you might as well just curl up in a cupboard somewhere and give up.

I'm lucky that I've been blessed with good looks and a winning personality but even if I hadn't, I would have made something of myself because that's the sort of person I am. And Gina hasn't done too badly at all, considering what she was like at school. She has her own business and this fabulous house and even though she's still a bit weird, that's her choice to be like that. Lots of people are weird or different nowadays; some people even pretend to be weird to make themselves seem more interesting.

I don't think that Gina is pretending, though, she really *is* weird.

We've actually spent quite a lot of time together in the evenings because I think that if you're living with someone then you should make the effort to get on with each other and be sociable. Although I did have a bit of an agenda; I wanted to become friends so she'd be amenable to me inviting my friends over or having them stay the night.

I've made a big effort even if she hasn't.

I've come to realise that our friendship, if you can call it that, is very one-sided. I've gone out of my way to be nice to her and to be friendly and believe me, I don't have to do that normally because usually people are desperately trying to be *my* friend and not the other way around. Gina's cold and standoffish and not at all easy to get on with and I find myself gabbling nonsense to try and fill the silence. It's getting to the point where I don't think I'm going to bother anymore. It's no hardship for me to stay in my rooms when I'm not out and about and her routine is like clockwork so she'd be dead easy to avoid.

She's very closed, too, as if her life is some big secret that no one's allowed to know about. I have to drag things out of her because she never, ever volunteers any information. I mean, what's the big secret? Who would I tell her boring stories to? No one, because they're not worth repeating they're so boring; not without a shed-load of embellishment, anyway.

I had to stifle a laugh when she was telling me about James, her boyfriend. As far as I can tell he hasn't actually stayed over yet, so does he even count as a boyfriend? I mean, come on, this is the twenty-twenties, not nineteen-seventy. I've no doubt he's a swotty, worthy type like her and wears a tweed jacket and brogues and talks earnestly about climate change and other boring stuff. He'd have to be like that to be interested in her because she's hardly head-turning or exciting or even *interesting*. She's not bad looking in a dull sort of way and she has a decent figure but my God, her clothes! She wears skirt suits and crisp white blouses and blocky-heeled court shoes as if she's fifty and not thirty-three. Honestly, some people have absolutely no idea. I could give her a makeover and make her look a hundred times better but do you know what, she doesn't deserve my help. And it would probably be wasted anyway, because her mind set is in the nineteen-seventies.

When I told her I was seeing someone she couldn't hide her disgust, although she tried. I actually wonder if she's still a virgin, what with the *taking things slowly with James* thing. Although she's been married, so she can't be a virgin. Unless she got divorced because the marriage wasn't consummated; nothing would surprise me about her. I dread to think what her reaction would be if she knew what my life was really like.

Although I haven't exactly lied to her; I *have* met someone special. Simon is absolute infatuated with me and he is rather gorgeous and rich too, so who knows. I'm not absolutely certain that I want to settle down so quickly with someone again but I won't tell him that, obviously, because I like to take my time while I consider my options. He's not the only man on the horizon because we're not exclusive, although he doesn't know this because I haven't actually told him because he hasn't asked. I have several *friends with benefits* and I refuse to feel guilty about it because I've been missing out for years and have an awful lot of catching up to do. I was totally faithfully to Hugh for all of our marriage – and that's more than most people can say. Nearly all of my friends have had at least one affair so I think I've been remarkably well-behaved and I'm not with Hugh now so I can do as I like.

From what I can remember when we were children, Gina hasn't changed very much; she was very quiet and reserved then and she's not much different now. I do wonder if that's why she's so cold towards me – is it because she remembers what a fool she made of herself that summer and she now feels embarrassed about it? I wouldn't blame her because if that was the case and if I was her, I wouldn't have let me rent the rooms. But she should have thought of that before she let me move in.

She'd stuck in my memory a bit from when we were kids because she was so weird, and when it dawned on me who she was when I came to look at the house, I had a tiny moment of indecision about taking the room. I didn't want her latching on and getting all moon-faced over me again like she did then. But I convinced myself it would be fine because I really wanted to live here and the rent was so cheap. As it's turned out I needn't have worried because she's quite the opposite and isn't very friendly at all.

It is a fault of mine that I'm too generous; that long-ago summer when Mummy, Daddy and I moved to Wetherton Avenue, I made the fatal mistake of letting Gina hang out with me because I felt sorry for her. Also, we'd moved too far away for me to see my old friends and having moved to a new place in the school holidays I was a bit bored and didn't really know anyone. For some reason, Gina got it into her head that we were going to be friends for life. If I'd known how weird she was and that she had no other friends I never would have let her tag along with me. Honestly, you try and do something kind and before you know it, you're lumbered with someone who you can't shake off. That's what happens when you're nice to people; they take advantage of your good nature. It's a lesson that I need to learn and remember for the future because Hugh has done exactly the same thing. I need to make sure that I don't keep repeating the same mistake over and over again.

The more I think about it, the more I think that I'm not going to bother trying to be Gina's friend anymore. I've spent far more time on her than she deserves and I'm not going to waste any more of my life bothering with her. Besides which, I don't actually like her very much; she's the same mousey

JOANNE RYAN

bore that she was when we were twelve.

I'm not asking about having my friends to stay over for the night, either, I'm just going to do it because I'm paying rent for my rooms so I can do what I like in them.

And anyway, Gina's so uptight and old maidish, she's hardly going to challenge me about it, is she?

CHAPTER EIGHT

Gina

I hate her.

Hate is a strong word but that's how I feel. Lissa can have any man that she wants – she's always telling me this herself – but she has to steal mine. I see now why she was always fishing for details of James; it was so she could track him down and take him for herself. I don't suppose she even really wants him – she's just taking him to hurt me.

I thought she was sorry about what she'd done to me all those years ago when she first came here but now, I realise that I was wrong. The strange look on her face that I took for regret was really because she'd enjoyed treating me badly all those years ago and wanted to do it again. People like her get their kicks out of ruining other's lives.

I curse the day that I let her back into my life.

Because people don't change, do they?

Unpleasant children invariably turn into unpleasant adults and I should have expected nothing less. She laughed at me with her friends all those years ago and she's laughing at me now. To her, other people are for amusement and game-play and for making her feel good about herself. I only have to look at the way she's treated her husband to know what sort of person she is. She talks about him as if he's a love-sick puppy who she can no longer be bothered with, not a man she was married to for years.

I should hate James, too, because he's the one who's cheating on me, but I can't bring myself to. What red-blooded man would be able to resist someone like Lissa flaunting and throwing themselves at them? Not many, I'm sure. If someone without any morals at all offers themselves on a plate then there aren't many men who would be strong enough to turn them down. James is as much of a victim in this as I am.

How I hate her.

* * *

I have no recollection at all of driving home after I left the gym and when I awake, I find myself lying on my bed fully dressed, still wearing my shoes and coat and the room in darkness. I've been lying here for what seems like forever with their kiss at the gym playing over and over in my head on a loop. When I can bear it no longer, I haul myself into an upright position and switch the bedside lamp on. Through blurred vision I eventually focus to see that the alarm clock on my bedside table is telling me that it's four-thirty in the morning.

Over eleven hours since I left the gym.

I lie back down and concentrate and try to remember what I did after I saw them. I remember walking back to the car on shaking legs and opening the door and practically falling into the seat. I can see myself sitting in the car in a state of shock and then.

Nothing.

A sudden vision of my mother's face pops into my head and I can hear her voice taunting me; *it's happening again*, she is saying, *the thing that we don't talk about, it's happening again*.

No, it's not. It's definitely not. I shake the thought of her away. I've had a shock, that's all. I simply drove home on automatic pilot and crashed out on my bed and cried myself to sleep. It's *nothing* like the last time.

My head is pounding but, in a bid to steady my mind I get up and cross the room on unsteady feet to pull the curtains closed across the window. I slip my feet out of my shoes and begin to pull my clothes off and throw them into a heap on the floor. I go into the bathroom and turn the shower on full blast and force myself to stand underneath the hot spray.

I just need to calm down and think things

through properly and everything will be okay.

I stand underneath the hot water and it slowly begins to ease the tension in my body; I lather shampoo into my hair and rigorously rub my scalp as if it will erase the sight of James kissing Lissa. I rinse my hair and add shampoo and then rinse again. I then work the conditioner through and rinse again. By the time I turn off the shower and dry myself off with the towel my fingers are starting to crinkle and the water is running cold but I'm feeling much better; calmer and more in control. I wrap a towel around my hair turban-style and dry myself and wrap a towel around me. I cross the bedroom and pick up my discarded clothes from the floor and return to the bathroom and drop them into the laundry basket. I go back into the bedroom, pick up my shoes and place them on the shoe rack at the bottom of my wardrobe. I take a clean pair of pyjamas from the drawer and put them on. I do these mundane tasks efficiently and tidily, as if doing things that I do every day will somehow erase the memory of James and Lissa and make this day like any other.

I'm starting to wonder if I might have over-reacted; maybe James and I can still work things out. If James admits that it was just a silly one-off mistake and he begs for my forgiveness then surely there is still hope for us. The more I think about it the more sure I become that I've over-reacted; behaved hysterically, almost. It was just one kiss, after all, which counts for nothing these days. It's a fact that I'm old-fashioned and not everyone has the same standards as me. Although I was sure that James was of the same mind-set as I, let's not forget that he's a man, and men think differently from women. What I see as a passionate kiss could be seen as a mere peck on the cheek by a man.

And men are weak; what man could resist a beautiful woman throwing herself at him? Because Lissa is mostly definitely beautiful on the outside even though inside her soul is as dark as the Devil's.

One kiss doesn't mean that they're having an affair and everyone is allowed one mistake, aren't they? I'm sure that there can't be many relationships that haven't had the occasional bump along the way.

I think a part of me has already decided that I shall forgive James, because I love him and he deserves a second chance. I won't let one kiss with that woman spoil what we have; I won't let her win. It all seems rather unreal now and I think that by constantly reliving it in my mind it's becoming more of a kiss than it really was.

It was one little kiss, that's all; that doesn't have to be the end of James and I.

I'm starting to feel better now; relieved that I've forgiven him and we can still see each other. Lissa, however, is another story. I will never forgive her and I will be asking her to leave my house immediately; she has betrayed and I will not have her living under my roof.

Five-thirty-five.

It's pointless going back to bed now as I won't be able to sleep because I must have slept for nearly eleven hours already. I shall make myself a cup of camomile tea and take stock of the situation and rehearse in my head what I'm going to say to Lissa.

As I pad down the landing towards the stairs, I pass Lissa's room. The door is closed and I can't stop myself from stopping and putting my ear to the door and listening.

What if she has James in her room? What if it's more than just one kiss? What if he's in her bed right now making love to her?

Before I can stop myself and without thinking, I turn the door handle and silently open her door. I peer through the gap in the doorway and as my eyes adjust to the gloom, I can make out the outline of her double bed underneath the window.

Relief floods through me when I see that James is not in her bed. How stupid was I to think that he would actually cheat on me with her; a peck on the cheek is one thing but he would never jump into bed with her even if she's offering herself up for sex. I feel slightly disgusted with myself for thinking so little of him.

But then it hits me; James is not in her room but nor is Lissa.

And I have to ask myself; if she's not in her bed, then where is she?

* * *

'Giving notice?' I echo, staring at Susie in disbelief.

'Yes,' Susie says, in a clipped tone. 'Two weeks' notice as of today which I shall take as annual leave as it's due to me. Today will be my last day.'

'Buy why?' I ask. 'I thought you were happy here.'

'I'm sorry,' Susie says, avoiding looking at me. 'I have personal reasons.'

I watch her walk out of my office and back into reception and try to understand why everything in my life appears to be falling apart. I came into the office early, determined to put thoughts of Lissa and James from my mind and catch up on some paperwork before I needed to go out for my appointments. I was doing well, too, until Susie dropped her bombshell. She arrived at nine o'clock as usual and for some reason she seemed surprised to see me. I felt that there was an atmosphere once she arrived but I couldn't quite put my finger on what was wrong. I told myself that it was me and that after the previous evening's events I was simply projecting my anxiety onto Susie. With hindsight of course, she was obviously feeling uncomfortable because she intended giving me notice.

She made us both a cup of coffee but when she brought mine in, she didn't linger for a chat but went straight back out to her desk. We don't normally have long conversations or anything like that but I'll always try to have a word or two of polite chit-chat with her every morning before she starts work.

I heard the postman bring the post in at ten o'clock and she was chatting to him just like she always did and quite honestly, I never thought too much about her reticence with me because I had other things on my mind. We've always had a good working relationship but I try not to get too friendly because she is an employee and not a friend. I've had a string of receptionists and it doesn't pay to get too familiar with them otherwise they start taking liberties. She dropped the bombshell of her resignation when she brought the post in to me.

I'll have to ring an agency to get a temporary receptionist and I feel rather annoyed with Susie; she may think that *personal reasons* is good enough but I don't. She's been here for nearly a year and it's a bit much that I have to accept her using her annual leave instead of working her notice. If I'd wanted to dismiss her, I would have had to give her a month's notice.

I'll also have to use a different agency than the last one as the dispute with them still hasn't been resolved to my satisfaction. Quite honestly, it's all a bit much on top of the James and Lissa situation and I could do without the hassle. I know that I've made the decision to forgive James but I want to give it more thought to make absolutely certain that I'm making the right decision. Now that Susie has done this and given me something else to sort out.

The longer I sit and think about it the more I decide that I'm not going to be dictated to by Susie. I'm going to have it out with her; if she wants to leave then she can work the months' notice that's in her contract or I'm not going to pay her. She has no right to march in here and tell me that she's leaving today.

I ponder what would be the best way to do it; do I call her in here or go into reception and ask her? I decide to call her into my office because if I go out to her, I'm going to have to hover around her desk while I speak to her and I'll feel awkward. If I call her in here, she can sit down and I'll feel more comfortable.

'Susie,' I call, in what I hope is a friendly way. 'Could you pop in for a moment please?'

My request is met with silence and I wonder if she's going to pretend she hasn't heard. I often call to her like this when I need a document from her filing cabinet and she's never ignored me before. I'm about to repeat my request when she appears in the doorway. She makes no attempt to come into the office and stands looking at me.

'Could you come in and sit down for a moment, please?'

She doesn't answer, or smile, but walks in and sits down on the chair in front of my desk.

'Susie, I wanted to see if I could help. I really

don't want you to leave and if you need to take some time off to sort out your personal problems, I'd much rather you did that than give in your notice.'

She looks down at her hands for a moment and then looks up at me unsmilingly.

'I'm sorry, Gina, but I have to leave.'

'But why?' I ask. 'I'm sure we can work something out. Leaving is a bit drastic, isn't it? I've no wish to pry into your personal life but as I've just said, if you need time off it's not a problem.'

Susie sighs and stares at me.

'Okay,' she says. 'I didn't want to have to do this but the real reason I'm leaving is because of you.'

'Me?' I ask, in complete shock. 'Whatever do you mean?'

'It's impossible. You're impossible.' She stands up. 'I'm sorry but I'm leaving and that's the end of it.'

'But...' I start to say.

'And,' she says, 'Before you even think about trying to employ anyone else, I'd advise you to sort yourself out before it's too late.'

CHAPTER NINE

Gina

I sit in stunned silence and watch Susie walk back through to reception. I have no idea what she's talking about and gradually the shock begins to turn to anger. How dare she say I'm impossible! I've been an extremely considerate boss to her and have never micro-managed her or expected her to do anything that wasn't in her job description. Quite often on a Friday afternoon I'll let her leave an hour early if we're not busy and I've always been accommodating about time off for doctor and dentist appointments.

I push the chair back and stand up and try to ignore the tremble in my legs as I do so. I've had nothing to eat since yesterday lunchtime as I couldn't face anything but the effects of the lack of food hit me; I feel light-headed and nauseous. I take a deep breath and then walk around the desk and out into the reception office.

I stand in front of Susie's desk and watch as she empties her personal belongings from the drawers into a cardboard box.

'I thought it best if I go now,' she says, head bent over the drawer. 'I can't really see the point in staying until the end of the day.'

'And were you going to tell me,' I hear myself ask in a cutting tone. 'Or were you just going to vanish whilst expecting me to pay you your two weeks holiday pay?'

She takes the last item from the drawer and slams it shut.

'That's up to you, Gina,' she snaps, without looking at me. 'But if you don't pay me it won't be the first time, will it?'

'What are you talking about?' I ask. 'I've always paid you, even when you've been off sick.'

'One day sick,' she says, looking at me and scowling. 'That's all I've had. Just one. So don't try to make out that I haven't done my job properly because I have. Delaying paying me because I took one day off is not acceptable but I let it go the first time because I gave you the benefit of the doubt. Once is a mistake but twice is deliberate. *You're* the problem, Gina, not me.' She glares at me and I wonder where the pleasant, helpful Susie has gone. The anger that propelled me out of my office to confront her has vanished and now I just want things to go back to how they were.

'Susie. Please,' I say. 'If I've done something to upset you, please tell me because whatever it was, it wasn't intentional.'

She picks her coffee cup up from the desk and crams it into the shopping bag even though it still has the dregs of the last coffee she made inside it.

'I can't work here anymore because you're dragging me down and if I stay here, I'm worried that I won't be able to get another job.' She looks at me as if I'm supposed to know what she's talking about but I honestly have no idea. I stare at her blankly and she sighs.

'You're unprofessional. You miss appointments, you're never where you're supposed to be and you never tell me where you are. You don't answer your mobile phone. You promise to meet clients and then don't turn up.'

I stare down at her and she slams the box down on the desk.

'There are final demands for the rent and all the utilities and you promise you'll pay them but you never do and I'm the one that has to lie for you.' The words come out in a rush and her cheeks grow pink. 'It's embarrassing Gina; *I'm* embarrassed at making the same excuses for you over and over again. I don't know what you do all day but you're not doing what you should be doing and I can't take any more of it. I want to work for someone I can trust.'

❊ ❊ ❊

I made no further attempt to stop Susie from

leaving; she seemed determined that she was going and there was no way I was going to beg her to stay.

I feel rather hurt, if I'm honest. I thought that I'd been a considerate employer and I've tried my best to make the workplace a happy one but now she's thrown it all back in my face. After she'd left, I locked the office door and sat at her desk and went through the appointments diary and tried to make sense of what she'd said. As I sat there and studied the diary, I started to feel a bit better; when she told me her reasons for leaving, I immediately felt guilty and as if I'd done something wrong but the truth of it is that *she's* the one at fault. She hasn't been keeping me up to date with the scheduled meetings so any that I've missed are totally down to her. All of the meetings in the diary for last week were ones that I knew nothing about so *she* hasn't told *me*. I always tell her who I'm seeing each day so she's talking complete nonsense when she says she doesn't know where I am.

My suspicions about her were confirmed when I looked back through the rent and utilities file; she hasn't made one single payment to any of them for nearly a year so it's no wonder final demands have been arriving thick and fast.

She is the one at fault.

It is therefore no surprise that she was desperate to leave as she knew that her shortcomings were about to be discovered and she quite simply jumped before she was pushed. As to her accusation that I have deliberately withheld her salary – this is sheer nonsense as on the rare occasion that her salary payment failed it was due to a bank error and absolutely nothing to do with me.

Even knowing this, I still feel deeply unsettled; it is yet further proof of my poor lack of judgement of people's characters. I thought Susie was honest, trustworthy and hard-working and I have now discovered that she is the complete opposite.

Yet another person has let me down.

After I'd satisfied myself of Susie's mistakes and failings I returned to my desk and sat there for the rest of the afternoon and carefully considered my situation. I needed to find a new assistant and I needed to throw Lissa out of my house.

Two quite simple things that shouldn't take very much thinking about at all. Yet by the time I came to a decision about both of those things, I found myself sitting in a darkened office with no clue as to where the day had gone.

✽ ✽ ✽

I left work at my normal time and arrived home to an empty house. I immediately set about making a lasagne with a side of beetroot salad and some garlic bread. After careful thought I've realised my first, irrational thought that Lissa is trying to take James from me is most likely incorrect. Yes, she knows that I'm in a relationship with James but

James is a common name and she doesn't know his surname as I never shared that information with her. The only way she could know is if James told her about me. I'll know as soon as I see her if he has because she'll be unable to hide the triumph from her face. She'll want to brag and let me know that she's taken him from me.

My plan is to invite her to share dinner with me and as soon as her face tells me what I need to know I'll base what I do next on that. If she knows that James is *my* James then I'll throw her out onto the street immediately. And I mean throw; I'll take great pleasure in launching all of her belongings out of her window and onto the driveway.

If she *doesn't* know then once we've eaten, I'm going to ask her to move out and give her a week's notice. If she has no idea about myself and James, I don't want her to find out because I won't give her the satisfaction of knowing that she's hurt me. I've also decided not to tell James that I saw him with Lissa; the more I think about it, the more I think that Lissa was kissing *him* and not the other way around. I have no wish to drive him into her arms by coming across as the jealous girlfriend.

Lissa is an absolute trollop with a string of men on the go; I've heard her on her phone talking to them as I pass her rooms because she can never keep the doors closed like I've asked her to. Why she thinks I want to hear all about her sordid sex life and her numerous lovers bewilders me. Does she think she's clever sleeping with whoever she bumps into? I feel sorry for her ex-husband for being married to such a cheating slut.

I keep looking at the clock and wonder where she is; I want never to set eyes on her again but equally, I need her to come home so that I can either throw her out immediately or set the wheels in motion for her to move out. I try not to think about the fact that she may stay out until late because that would totally destroy my plan and I would then have to endure another sleepless night.

The lasagne is nearly cooked and I'm starting to think that she's not coming back when I hear the click of the front door being unlocked. I take a deep breath and paste a smile on my face that feels as if it will crack my face into two.

'Hi,' I call casually through the kitchen doorway. 'Good day?'

Lissa saunters along the hallway towards me, her high heels making a clicking noise on the parquet flooring. When she's gone, I'll no longer have to suffer her wearing outdoor shoes inside my house when I've specifically asked her not to.

'Not bad,' she says, leaning against the doorframe and folding her arms.

I look at her and hope that my smile doesn't look like the grimace that it feels. I study her face and can see no hint of triumph or mockery and at once I'm certain that she doesn't know about James. She wouldn't be able to contain herself if she did. If anything, she looks tired and fed-up and not her usual insufferable, bragging self. I'm not a violent person but right now I want to punch her in the face and pull her perfect hair out by the roots and drag her down onto the floor and repeatedly kick her. The strength of this feeling shocks me and I have to grip the tea towel tightly to stop myself from attacking her. I want to knock her teeth out and claw that pretty face into ribbons but I must stay calm or everything will unravel.

She cocks her head to one side and looks at me and there's the merest hint of a frown between her brows. I wonder if somehow, she's reading my mind.

'Just one of those days,' she says, with a sigh, dispelling my worries. 'My ex, Hugh, is being difficult. Why he can't just sign the divorce papers and fuck off is beyond me.'

I try to not to show my shock at her foul language; she rarely swears so he must have done something bad to rattle her. I feel a small glow of satisfaction which rapidly grows into something approaching happiness; everything is going to be alright. She doesn't know about me and James and of course she wouldn't, because he wouldn't do that to me after one silly little kiss, would he?

'Men, eh?' she says, with a shrug. 'Can't live with them, can't kill them.'

'Very true,' I say, with a laugh that sounds false even to my own ears. I see her glance over my shoulder and I know that she's spotted the salad on the table.

'Lasagne,' I say. 'I've made plenty if you want to join me.'

'Oh, yes please,' she says, sniffing the air. 'Smells divine.'

'It'll be ready in five minutes.' I pull two plates out from the cupboard and place them on the table. I take cutlery from the drawer and place it beside the plates and then take two wine glasses out of the cupboard and put them on the table.

'Fabulous,' she calls, disappearing along the hallway and up the stairs. 'I'll just visit the little girls' room and I'll be down.'

The little girls' room, ugh, I won't miss her saying that either. I take a bottle of red from the wine rack and open it. Yet again I'm supplying the wine and the food but this will be the very last time that she enjoys my hospitality so I'm prepared to be generous.

Besides which I need a drink myself.

I pour a glass and take several mouthfuls and as I feel the warmth of it running through my body I start to relax. I should have opened it sooner and let it breathe but I didn't want to tempt fate; if I'd opened it before she arrived then maybe she wouldn't have come home tonight.

I turn the oven off and take the lasagne out and put it on a mat in the centre of the table. It does look good; it's a shame that my stomach is churning and I won't enjoy it fully although there's no denying that I'm hungry. I take the garlic bread out of the oven and cut it into pieces and put it in a basket on the table next to the salad.

'Mmm, yum, looks delish,' Lissa's voice says, from behind me.

I sit down at the table and she comes around in front of me and drags the chair out opposite and flops into it. She's changed from her designer work clothes into baggy striped pyjamas and I can't help feeling disgusted with her. How can she take up my offer of dinner and arrive to eat it in pyjamas? Has she no manners at all?

'Please, help yourself.' I wave at the lasagne and she dives in with the spoon while I fill her wine glass and top mine up. I put the smallest portion of lasagne possible onto my plate followed by a helping of salad. I load up my fork and put it into my mouth where it feels as if I have a huge dry towel in my mouth. I chew and chew and chew and somehow, manage to swallow it down. Lissa is tucking into the lasagne with gusto and has already drunk half of her glass of wine. She takes no notice of me as I push the food around my plate with my fork rather than attempt to eat it.

'So have you started looking at houses yet?' I force myself to ask her once I've finished. We've eaten our meal in silence and I can't remember if this is normal or not; do we usually chat as we eat or do we wait until we've finished? I know that I'm being paranoid but I can't help it. Lissa doesn't answer straight away but puts her knife and fork down on the plate and pushes the empty plate into the middle of the table. All the lasagne is gone;

Lissa helped herself to seconds when I offered them and I'm surprised at how much she's eaten. Normally she picks at her food, which, I suppose, is how she keeps her perfect figure. Maybe her ex-husband really has upset her and this is comfort eating; for the second time this evening I feel a glow of satisfaction at something not going perfectly for her.

'No, not yet,' she replies. 'No point in looking until I know exactly how much I'm going to get.' She takes another swallow of wine before tipping the rest of the bottle into her glass.

'Oops,' she says. 'Greedy me, that's the last of it.'

I laugh but find that I can't look at her; I want to pick the knife up from my plate and drive it between her eyes and I fear that if I look at her face any longer that's exactly what I'll do. I look down at the table and blurt it out before I have a chance to stop myself.

'So, Lissa,' I say, in a shaky voice. 'I'm sorry if it's not convenient but I'm going to have to ask you to move out.'

CHAPTER TEN

Lissa

When I got back to the house, I opened the front door and the smell of garlic hit me; something was cooking in that kitchen and it smelt so good. I wondered if Gina was having the boyfriend round for a meal because she never usually bothered cooking just for herself. She'd always help herself to huge portions of anything I cooked but rarely cooks herself. I think if I wasn't here, she'd mostly live on takeaways because she's always happy to share one with me when I offer. She should look at her diet and take herself in hand now otherwise she'll balloon into a big fatty; I can see the signs, she's a natural pig who can't control her portion sizes.

She called out to me as I headed down the hallway and for once she sounded happy; definitely a boyfriend night, I decided. Maybe, I thought, she's on a promise and is finally going to let him into her bed. I wondered if I'd finally get to meet him to confirm my suspicion that he's as dull and boring as she is.

Maybe, the thought crossed my mind, I'd hang around and flirt with him just to annoy her; show him what a real woman is like. Although if he's the same as her he'll be severely socially retarded and wouldn't have a clue how to respond. Maybe he hasn't tried to get into her bed because he hasn't got a shag in him. Because let's face it, he can't be up to much if he's lumbered with her. I'm not usually so spiteful but today has been the day from hell so I gave full vent to my nasty thoughts.

I was gob-smacked when she asked me if I'd had a good day, I'm normally the one instigating conversation and I'd pretty much decided that I wasn't going to bother anymore. Let there be awkward silences and atmospheres because I wasn't going to make any more effort with someone who obviously couldn't be bothered to make an effort with me. She caught me unawares and I can't remember exactly what I said but it was something about Hugh being a pain which I wouldn't normally admit to. I'm pretty sure that I dropped the f-bomb too, because I remember that she looked pretty disgusted. Honestly, I wanted to laugh and tell her to go and live in a church or become a nun or something but I stopped myself because I didn't want to say anything that I'd then have to apologise for. I am not in an apologising mood today and most definitely not to a sour-faced, frigid spinster.

I was even more shocked when she offered me dinner and once I'd accepted, I quickly ran upstairs and got into my pj's before coming back down. She'd actually got the wine out too without me having to drop massive hints, which made me wonder what her agenda was because she's usually so tight-fisted and miserable.

I wasn't really in the best of moods to have dinner with her because Hugh is being such an arse. Somehow, he's got wind of the fact that I'm seeing other guys and he's gone all holier than thou and is behaving as if we're still married. It's really none of his business who I see now that we're getting divorced but he's got it into his head that I was cheating on him when we together. I told him that of course I wasn't and hand on heart, I never cheated on him, but he refused to believe me. I was a bit shocked that he was being so self-righteous and horrible to me because I can usually sweet talk him round to my way of thinking. Until now our telephone conversations have consisted of him telling me that he still loves me and begging me to give him another chance.

Not so today.

No, today he told me that he'd instructed his solicitor to scrutinise our financial affairs and to make sure that any outstanding balances on our own personal credit cards or loans are treated separately from our dual finances. This is not good news for me; Hugh has *no* credit cards or loans because he's completely boring and rarely buys designer clothes or other personal stuff, whereas I have three cards all maxed out to the hilt plus a personal loan that he doesn't know about. I took the loan out to clear the credit cards but never got around to it because I ended up spending it on some rather expensive beauty treatments. Looking as good as I do requires regular maintenance and it isn't achieved by using supermarket cosmetics and cutting my own hair. I'm furious at Hugh because it means that my share of the settlement is going to be much smaller than I'd anticipated. I'm going to have to rein in the spending considerably or marry someone else who's extremely rich. I'll have to lower my sights when I start looking for houses or curtail my spending; neither option is attractive.

I could order my solicitor to contest this but realistically I know that it would be futile. Also, have you seen how much solicitors charge just to write a letter or make a telephone call? Honestly, being a divorce solicitor is practically a licence to print money and they don't actually do anything except cause trouble and arguments so that they can charge even more money to sort out the arguments *they* created. And I can't even moan to Mummy and Daddy because they'd want to know why I have so much debt and get all sanctimonious about it. They don't understand about having to look good and Mummy gets all funny if she thinks I've had Botox or fillers; she has this weird idea that it's *surgery*. She says that you shouldn't put chemicals into your body as it's bad for you; I think she forgets that she spent years of her life cooking underneath an indoor sun bed to keep up her perma-tan. It's only now that she's hit her sixties that she's started to age gracefully so maybe she ought to remember how she used to be.

Although I *have* had a tiny bit of surgery which she doesn't know about but I'm certainly not going to tell her. Cosmetic surgery doesn't come cheap but who wants to have boobs that flap around like rabbit's ears? I don't – which is why I had them perked up a little bit before they actually needed it so that they never get to that point.

Hugh has never been so mean to me before and I'm having a hard time understanding it. The only thing that I can think of is that he's got another woman, because he'd never have thought of this on his own. If another woman has got her hooks into him, she'll be making sure that he doesn't give me a penny more than I'm entitled to and keeps his money for himself.

How can I be so sure of this?

Because it's exactly what I would do if I was the new woman.

All of this was the back of my mind when I sat down to eat Gina's lasagne. I wasn't feeling exactly sociable so I didn't instigate any conversation and we ate the whole meal in silence. The lasagne was good though, I'll give her that, and the garlic bread, too. I could tell that she was agitated about something because she pushed her food around her plate but didn't actually eat anything. I knew there must have been an ulterior motive behind her invitation to dinner but I was still surprised that she came out with it so bluntly because I didn't think she had it in her.

She wants me to leave.

Not immediately, she said, as if she was doing me a massive favour, she would give me a week to move my things out.

I was fuming but I didn't give her the satisfaction of letting her know. I asked her; do you need me to move out because James is moving in?

She said he was but she couldn't meet my eyes when she said it so I'm sure she's lying. I think she just wants me to leave because she can't cope with sharing a house with anyone else because she's a social retard. Her so-called boyfriend hasn't even spent one night here so he's hardly going to move in with her, is he? I'm beginning to wonder if she even has a boyfriend or if he's a figment of her imagination.

I told her that a week's notice might be pushing it a bit and she said that as I usually stayed out several nights a week couldn't one of my friends put me up? The cheek of her; she's even checking up when I'm actually sleeping here as if she's my mother or something. I could tell by the way she said *friends* that she really meant men and she couldn't keep the disgust from showing on her face. Just because I choose to have sex with more than one man doesn't make me a slut; men are allowed to play the field so why shouldn't I? It's not as if I'm hurting anyone. I made an excuse and left the kitchen and went up to my rooms then because I knew that if I stayed, I'd end up having a huge row with her and telling her exactly what I think of her and then I'd have to move out even sooner.

I have options and there are several places that I could move into, because unlike her I have friends and family, but whether I want to is another matter.

I could move back in with Hugh; the house is half mine and I'm perfectly entitled to live there. If I did this I could also find out for sure if he has another woman and it would cramp his style massively if he's been having her stay over. It would also be cheaper as he's paying all the bills and the mortgage so I'd actually be better off than I am now. The drawback with this is that he'd know exactly what I get up to as well and it would cramp *my* style and I'm not comfortable with that at all. It's bad enough having Gina-the-spinster watching my every move, let alone Hugh-the-ex-husband. I'd have to keep my men friends at arm's length and I know that Hugh would be questioning me every time I left the house or stayed out overnight.

So that's a definite no; there are always my parents but I think that would be even worse than living with Hugh so that's ruled out, too.

Which leaves Simon.

He's the perfect man; rich, handsome and absolutely mad about me. He's been begging me to move in with him almost from the minute that I met him and I haven't yet found anything about him that I don't like; he's funny and charming, takes me to fabulous restaurants and always buys me beautiful gifts.

So maybe I should move in with him.

But I don't want to; not yet.

I've only had a short taste of freedom since I told Hugh our marriage was over and I'm loath to give it up just yet. For the first time in years, I'm actually enjoying myself; I'm enjoying dating different men and having sex with a man if I so choose. I'm having fun and I don't want it to stop. I don't want to move in and settle down with one man just yet; maybe I never will, I really don't know.

Which leaves me with looking for a house-share again.

As annoying and ridiculous as Gina is, her house is fabulous. The chances of me finding anything remotely as nice as this house are about a million-to-one. The thought of sharing a dirty, shabby house with a bunch of undesirables makes me want to vomit.

So, what do I do?

It's a dilemma; and until I've decided I'm just going to sit tight and consider my options.

No matter what Gina says.

She can fucking wait until I'm good and ready.

CHAPTER ELEVEN

Gina

I was dreading telling Lissa that she had to move out but I shouldn't have worried; it went much better than I expected. I feel relieved that the deed is done and I'll make sure that I avoid seeing her for her last week here. She asked if James was moving in and I said he was – she obviously does listen sometimes because she must have remembered that I told her we were thinking of moving in together the first time she came here.

I had a surge of anger when she said James's name; as if somehow by speaking his name she had ownership of him. She has absolutely no idea that the James she threw herself at outside the gym was *my* James. It felt surreal to sit and talk about him to her and in a way, it made me feel almost powerful because I knew and she didn't. I'm certain that she doesn't know because she wouldn't be able to contain herself from bragging about it to me so that she could cause me pain and belittle me.

She didn't linger for very long after we'd finished eating; the atmosphere felt a little awkward after I'd asked her to leave and she disappeared upstairs saying that she had some sorting out to do. She left me to do the clearing up and it struck then that I've always been the one clearing up after a meal or a takeaway, so as well as being a slut she's also lazy.

I was pleased to see the back of her and breathed a huge sigh of relief that she would soon be gone and my life could return to normality. I'm not quite sure what I would have done if she had made a fuss about moving out; I feared that the violent thoughts that kept crossing my mind as we ate dinner could easily become a reality if she provoked me.

Everything will be fine now, I assured myself as I loaded the dishwasher and wiped the worktops. Seven more days and she would be gone from my life forever. Nevertheless, I couldn't sleep last night and when I awoke this morning I felt as if I had been battling with someone or something for the whole night and rather than feeling refreshed, I felt exhausted.

Which is why I stayed at home today.

I should have gone into the office but I simply

couldn't face it after the showdown with Susie yesterday. The thought of sitting there alone depressed me intensely so I took the easy option and didn't go. I sent a text message to a client who was due to come in and cancelled my appointment for this afternoon. I felt awful for doing something so unprofessional but I couldn't bear the thought of pretending that I'm fine and nothing is wrong. Rather worryingly, the client never replied to my text and I have a niggling feeling that I may have lost his business but I can't do anything about that now; I'll sort it out next week.

I did feel bad about Mrs Heppleton; she'll turn up for her Friday chat like she always does and the office will be locked and she'll wonder what on earth is going on. I can't do anything about it now because she doesn't use text; I could phone her but honestly, I don't have the energy for having a conversation with anyone.

The last few days have rather taken it out of me and I need peace and quiet to recover. Tomorrow is Saturday so I have three whole days with no work to worry about and I'm going to use it to pamper myself and get some well-earned rest. Lissa is always out and about at weekends so I should be able to easily avoid her. I also don't imagine that she'll be seeking out my company now I've given her notice to leave.

I texted James and told him that I'm away at a spa weekend with some of my girlfriends this weekend so I won't be able to see him. I simply can't face seeing him at the moment even though I love him deeply. I fear if I see him now, I'll say something that I regret and there'll be no going back. I need space for the picture of Lissa kissing him to fade; I need to get some perspective on things. I hate lying to him but I need time to sort myself out.

The cleaner hasn't turned up at all this week for some inexplicable reason and she's ignored my text messages. Quite unacceptable behaviour in my opinion, so as well as a new receptionist I will also be looking for a new cleaner. It's true that once one thing goes wrong, everything else seems to follow.

Intent on keeping myself occupied and determined not to mope, I threw myself into cleaning the house – not Lissa's rooms, obviously. Once I'd finished cleaning and dusting, I vacuumed the carpets in the entire house. By the time I'd finished I was sweating and felt as if I'd done an intense work-out at the gym. I felt a lot better, mentally, than when I started and more like my old self; the person I was before that damned woman moved into my house and tried to ruin my life.

I then treated myself to a long soak in the bath with my favourite bubbles and I'd just got dressed when I heard the door-bell ring. I came downstairs, wondering who on earth it could be; I wasn't expecting any deliveries and I knew that it couldn't be a delivery for next door because I've made it quite clear to my neighbours that I've no wish to take in their endless Amazon deliveries. By the time I'd reached the hallway the ringing door-bell was accompanied by repeated rattling of the letter-box flap and I was furious that someone thought that they could demand that I open the door in this way. I'd pretty much decided that I wasn't going to answer it when I saw through the opaque glass of the door that someone was attempting to stick a sheet of paper to the other side of the glass.

I stood at the bottom of the stairs for a moment, absolutely infuriated that someone would think they had a right to stick something on my front door. I took a deep breath to calm myself and then marched across the hallway, unlocked the door and yanked it open to be confronted by a very large man wearing a black puffer jacket and holding a clipboard. A similarly dressed man stood behind him and my earlier anger dissipated and I tried very hard not to feel intimidated.

'What,' I demanded, loudly. 'Do you think you're doing?'

'Georgina Moray?' he asked, completely unperturbed by my shouting at him.

'And who wants to know?' I demanded of him.

'Darren Richards. Certificated enforcement officer.' He held up a driving licence sized plastic card in front of me and stared at me unsmilingly. I glared back at him and made no attempt to read his card.

'I have no idea who you are but please get off my property,' I stated, haughtily. I made to shut the front door but he put a huge boot-clad foot in the way making it impossible to close. I looked up at him in shock.

'The bailiffs, love,' he said, in a softer tone. 'We're the bailiffs, and we've come to collect your debt.'

✽ ✽ ✽

Despite their rough appearance, Darren and Geoff, as I discovered the other bailiff was called, were surprisingly polite whilst they informed me that they would be collecting goods to the value of three-thousand-two-hundred and fifty pounds.

Darren, in particular, was most concerned when my legs began to shake and I thought I was going to faint. He put his huge arm around me and helped me to the kitchen where I sat at the table and wondered what on earth had happened. It says something about my state of mind that I allowed a strange man to handle me in such a way. He even offered to make me a cup of tea before he began an inventory of my belongings. He asked if there was anyone I wanted them to contact to come and sit with me whilst they carried out their duties and this quickly brought me to my senses. I wanted no witnesses to the embarrassment of having a bailiff visit my house, even if it was a mistake.

According to Darren and Geoff, final demand

letters and warnings of this visit have been sent to me many times over the preceding months and I have ignored them all. The sheet of paper that Darren was attaching to the front door was a warning of their next visit when they would be accompanied by a policeman and a locksmith to force entry. The debt that I owe is for unpaid council tax bills from this house and my previous home – plus the enormous amount of fees that have accumulated because I've failed to pay.

I don't recall receiving any final demands but this is not an excuse that they will accept; I have to give them the money in cash or they will take goods from my home to the value of the debt. I immediately thought of Lissa; has she opened my post and deliberately thrown the letters away to cause mischief? I would not be surprised at anything she did but realistically, she hasn't been living here for very long and according to the bailiffs I would have received letters long before she moved in. Not that it matters now; I have to pay and it has to be today.

I told them that I would pay them in cash if they could wait whilst I paid a visit to the bank. Darren told me that Geoff would stay in the house while he accompanied me to the bank.

I felt like a prisoner.

He insisted on driving me in the transit van that they arrived in and when we pulled up in the car park at the rear of the bank, I was surprised that he got out and came with me into the bank.

There was a queue, of course, and we stood next to each other in silence while we waited for the extremely slow bank cashier to serve each person. When I finally arrived at the counter, Darren stood slightly behind me whilst I asked for the three-thousand-two-hundred and fifty pounds, averting his head when I put my card in the card machine and punched in my pin number. I always have a healthy bank balance and have at least three or four-thousand pounds in my account so I knew that it wouldn't be a problem.

Except that it was.

The card machine made a beeping noise and the cashier looked at it and frowned and then tapped a few keys on her keyboard and frowned some more. She then looked up and informed me that I wouldn't be able to withdraw any money today as my account was overdrawn. She then further advised me that as I'd exceeded my maximum overdraft, I would be unable to use my debit card until I had deposited sufficient funds to cover the overdraft.

I could feel my face flushing scarlet but managed to mumble that there must be some mistake. The cashier's face hardened and she assured me that there was no mistake but if I wished to speak to the manager then that could be arranged. I told her not to bother and stormed out of the bank with Darren Richards in my wake and I stood silently as he unlocked the van. I climbed into the passenger seat and without another word he started the engine and we headed back to my house.

It began immediately once we were back inside the house; Darren went into each room with his clipboard and valued all of the items therein. Many items were exempt as they had finance on them; my bespoke three piece suite, my Bang and Olufsen music centre and all of the furniture in one of the bedrooms that is kitted out as my office to name but a few. Thankfully, my car has outstanding finance on it so they couldn't take that otherwise I would have no way of running my business.

They took the television from the lounge and from my bedroom but that wasn't enough to cover the debt. We arrived outside Lissa's room and Geoff had already clomped his way in before I had a chance to tell him that none of the contents were mine. He immediately spotted a large jewellery box on the chest of drawers that was full to the brim with assorted necklaces and bracelets. He made a bee-line for it but once there he ignored the jewellery box and picked up a watch lying next to it. He picked up the watch and studied it, turning it over in his hands before passing it to Darren.

'Looks real to me, boss,' he said to Darren.

Darren looked carefully at the watch, feeling the weight of it in his hand.

'Be worth more if we had the box and certificate. Do you have it?' he asked, turning to me.

I shook my head mutely and he sighed in disappointment.

'Shame. You could have had both tellies back but as it is, if you let me have this Rolex, I'll give you back the one from the lounge.'

I stood dumbly looking at him and wondered when I might wake up from this nightmare. The silence stretched until eventually Darren spoke.

'What's it to be? Do we take the watch or do you want us to keep looking and take something else?'

The watch belonged to Lissa and I had no right to give it to them; besides which she'd be bound to notice that it was missing. I needed to tell them that it didn't belong to me so he could put it back and carry on looking in the rest of the house.

I took a deep breath and looked at Darren.

'Take the watch,' I said.

CHAPTER TWELVE

Gina

When I awoke this morning, I thought that I was at Wetherton Avenue. In that strange time between sleeping and being fully awake, I was convinced that I could hear the sound of my mother and father arguing and it was only when I found myself standing on the landing at the top of the stairs that I fully woke up. I'd somehow got out of bed and walked there without even realising; almost sleep-walking. I know that I did it because I thought that I'd be able to hear better from the top of the stairs even though I knew what they were saying would be bad. Strangely, once I realised that I was dreaming I felt a sense of disappointment. I couldn't quite understand why as I haven't seen my parents for years and have absolutely no desire to as I consider them dead to me. I put these strange feelings down to the turmoil of the last couple of days.

I felt disorientated and almost detached from reality and I resorted to standing at my bedroom window for quite some time in order to ground myself. I looked out over the front and concentrated; that's my car, this is my house and it's eight-thirty on a Saturday morning and I'm thirty-three years old. Eventually, I started to feel better but it was a very strange start to the day.

In desperation for a good night's sleep last night, I took a sleeping tablet from a packet that I found at the back of one the kitchen cupboards. I have no idea where the sleeping tablets came from but they had my name on them, although I couldn't make out the date of the prescription as the ink had faded. Maybe this was the reason that I didn't wake fully and had the bizarre yearning for the past. Although it may also be that when I went to bed last night, thoughts of my mother and father weighed heavily on my mind.

I think, if I'm completely honest with myself, that something's not quite right with me. The visit from the bailiffs yesterday shook me to the core and although I tried to tell myself that it was just a mistake and I'd forgotten to pay my council tax bill, I knew that there was more to it than that. The bailiff's visit, coupled with Susie's resignation, made me realise that it's unlikely that other people are making multiple mistakes over unpaid bills while I have made none.

After the bailiff's had left, I paced around the house for several hours and then forced myself go upstairs to my office. I needed to know how bad things really were because the sensible part of me knew that I would have received the final demands and that I must have put them somewhere. They couldn't have *all* gone astray or not been sent so I searched my files of papers and my filing cabinet but could find nothing. I knew I'd find nothing before I even started but I continued with the pointlessness of it in a bid to delay the inevitable.

I put the last box file back on the shelf and sat on the swivel chair and stared at my desk. I always lock the drawers but leave the key dangling in the lock. Pretty pointless, as locking it and leaving the key to hand makes no sense but there is nothing of any value in there so I have no idea why I lock it at all. I pulled out the top drawer and a few pens and pencils rattled around an unused notebook. I pushed the drawer back in and stared at the bottom drawer; the bottom drawer is big enough to suspend files in and has runners to hang them from but I never use it for this as I have a filing cabinet. The only thing I keep in that drawer is paper for my printer. I stared at the drawer and before I could change my mind, I yanked it wide open.

It was full.

Not of blank paper but of letters; brown and white envelopes, some with *final demand* stamped in red across them, or *important – do not ignore;* dozens of them; so many that they spilled out onto the floor once the drawer was open.

None of them were opened.

I slammed the drawer shut and closed my eyes for a moment as if I could make them disappear before slowly opening the drawer again. Of course, the envelopes were still there.

How did they get there?

The only possible answer is that I put them there. I reached down and picked up a brown envelope from the top and slit it open. It was a letter from the council telling me that unless I settled the unpaid council tax owing within seven days the debt would be passed to the county court.

It was dated two months ago.

I pulled out another envelope and slit it open and continued to do this, trance-like, until the drawer was empty and the waste-paper bin was full of envelopes and the desk was covered in letters. I then set about sorting the letters into piles, depending on whom they were from and then sorted the piles into date order. Once I was finished, I had nine piles of paper on my desk. There were final demands for my car loan, the sofa and music system as well as for my new laptop and my credit cards. Most frightening of all, there were letters from the bank advising me that I was in arrears with my mortgage and to contact them at my earliest convenience to speak to them. This letter was dated two months previously.

The oldest letter that I found was from four months ago; which was only three months after I moved in.

I tried to think back over the last seven months since I moved into the house to understand what had happened; how could I have been hiding these letters and continuing my life as if nothing had happened? How could I have been lying to myself like this?

Is this why Susie gave her notice in? Had I been doing the same at work and ignoring the fact that my business was struggling?

Determined to face facts, I opened up my laptop on the desk and when the welcome screen appeared I navigated to my business bank account. I clicked on the account button and held my breath while the page loaded.

Overdrawn.

The figures danced in front of my eyes and I took a deep breath; this was no time for histrionics, I had to face facts and deal with the problem. I leaned forward to study the figures. My business account was nearly a thousand pounds overdrawn and looking back over the last few months, I could see that my income has dwindled to almost nothing.

Susie was right; it wasn't her fault at all, it was mine.

I closed down my business account and opened up my personal current account; I needed to know the whole problem if I was going to try and sort it out. I already knew that my account was overdrawn from the bank cashier but I didn't know by how much; the screen appeared and I saw that I'd exceeded my personal overdraft of two thousand pounds by over five hundred pounds. No wonder the bank manager wanted to see me.

I closed down the screen and looked around the desk; I'm a financial adviser, I told myself, I should be able to sort this out if anyone can. I'd have to contact every one of the debtors and arrange some sort of minimal payment but in order to pay any sort of regular payment I needed to generate more income.

I could get another lodger.

The thought popped into my head and I laughed out loud like a loon. I hated the one I had so why would I get another? Besides, I would need more than one lodger to make the slightest dent in the mountain of debt that I'd created.

I needed to tackle the problem and I felt defeated before I'd even started and that's without even beginning to understand how it can have happened. I had a sudden yearning to hear James's voice; how stupid I'd been to lie and tell him that I was away for the weekend at a spa with atrociously bad mobile reception. How could I tell him that I was up to my eyes in debt? What would he think of me?

What would he think of me if he found out that I was a thief, that I'd stolen my lodger's watch to pay my debtors?

It was despicable, but not the worst thing that I'd done.

No, the worst thing was that I'd stolen from her and I didn't even care.

She deserved it.

* * *

After breakfast this morning I went back up to the office to make a start. I made a spreadsheet with a list of each debtor and the amount and put the letters into files. I thought that actually sorting and detailing the figures would make me feel better but it didn't; the actual amount that I calculated that I owe was so high that there's no way I'll ever be able to pay it off.

I'll have to sell the house.

There is nothing else for it.

Hopefully, if I sell the house, by the time everything is paid off I'll have enough left over for a deposit on a small flat.

That's supposing, of course, that I can ever get another mortgage.

There's no point in trying to contact anyone over the weekend so I'll start making the calls on Monday to try and make some sort of payment plan with my debtors.

I will also have to look for a job.

The rent is months overdue on the office and my paying clients have dwindled to next to nothing; I realise now why the client that I cancelled yesterday didn't bother to reply. Like the others, he has gone elsewhere. I can still keep on my few remaining clients and work from home but I need to find some other way of supplementing my income.

It was dark by the time I'd finished sorting and putting everything onto a spreadsheet and I felt exhausted. I realised that I hadn't eaten or drunk anything since breakfast so I've made some tea and toast to prevent myself from getting a headache and feeling even worse.

I finish the tea and toast but I still feel sick; most likely I will feel like this for a very long time. I close the lounge door just in case Lissa decides to come home although that's extremely unlikely on a Saturday night; she will be no doubt be spending the night with one of her men friends.

I lie down on the sofa and switch the television on that the bailiffs nearly claimed and flick through the channels. I need to find something to watch so I can think of something other than my mountain of debt and how it can have happened. I refuse to think about how it happened, it just has. I took my eye off the ball and let things slip, that's all.

My thoughts naturally turn to James and I imagine his soft brown eyes and his beautiful smile. Thank God I have him, otherwise I seriously think that my life wouldn't be worth living. Would I be able to go on without him? I don't like to think about it but I already know the answer. I'm not blaming him for Lissa the trollop's behaviour. James and I are two halves of the same person; we don't even need to speak to one another to know how we feel, just one look at each other and we know. I may have made a mess of my finances and business but thankfully, we still have each other. You can replace money, I tell myself, but not love.

I'm going to have to tell him about the debt, but not yet, I'll wait until a payment plan is sorted and it's all straight in my mind. I yearn to ring him just to hear his voice but I don't want him to know that I've lied about being away for the weekend. I've never lied to him before and this is the first and last time; I will never lie to him again.

My mobile screen leaps into life and the jaunty ring-tone mocks my sombre mood. I pick it up from the floor beside me to cancel the call but as I glance at the screen, my heart lifts when I see who's calling. James is calling me even though he knows it's unlikely he'll get through. I feel suddenly happy; I may have lost everything financially but love is worth far more than money. He knows, somehow James knows that I need him and he's calling to tell me he loves me. This is proof that our love is almost telepathic and I have tears in my eyes as I press the button to answer.

'Darling,' I say, choking back the tears. 'It's so good to hear your voice.'

CHAPTER THIRTEEN

Lissa

'**M**ove in with me.'

I snuggle closer to Simon and pull the quilt up over my shoulders. It's Saturday morning and we're lying in his super-king-sized bed having just enjoyed some sizzling sex. Maybe I should move in; he's pretty much perfect in the bedroom department and has oodles of money, so why wouldn't I?

Because I just don't know if I'm ready to settle for one man, that's why. Hugh seemed perfect to start with and the sex was amazing but once we'd bought a house and were living as a couple life became predictable and dull. I know if I moved in with Simon that once the novelty wears off, we'll be like every other couple and settle into comfort mode. In no time at all he'll be breaking wind in front of me and I won't bother to shave my legs in the winter.

I don't know if I want that yet; I don't know if I *ever* want that again.

'You're ignoring me,' he says, stroking my hair.

I sit up and look at him.

'I'm not,' I say, pouting. 'I just need to think about it for a while. We've not known each other for very long, have we?'

He pulls me close to him and kisses me and I feel his hand sliding downwards.

'I've known you long enough,' he murmurs.

'Hey, cheeky,' I say, pushing his hand away and sitting up. 'Let a girl catch her breath.'

He laughs his deep laugh.

'I can't help it if I can't keep my hands off you, can I? Is it my fault you're so gorgeous that all I want to do it rip your clothes off and have my wicked way with you?'

I laugh and snuggle back down and rest my head on his chest and try to think logically. Maybe I should move in; just because I move in with him it doesn't mean I have to stay here forever, does it? It's not as if I'm getting married to him; if I decide it's not working it'll be a simple case of packing my bags and leaving. It's not the same as moving on from Hugh; we have all the intertwined finances and the house to contend with which means costly solicitors making it more difficult. There would be none of that with Simon, I'd still be free to leave at any time I liked.

Maybe I could move in for a while and see how things go. If I change my mind about Simon I can move out and buy my own place once my share of the money is through. It's not as if I'd be committing to him forever. Also, living with Simon would be heaps cheaper than a house share or paying a huge deposit and renting a flat on my own. Knowing how generous Simon is I could probably live here for free because I can't see him allowing me to pay for anything.

But I can't ignore the niggle at the back of my head that says don't do it. I can't help feeling that if I move in, I'm somehow giving in and relying on a man again when I've barely moved out from living with Hugh and I don't want to do that.

'Of course,' Simons says, determined not to let it drop. 'You'd have to give up all your other boyfriends if you moved in with me.'

I laugh but I know that he means it because I can hear the jealousy in his voice. I've never discussed my other men friends with him but before we became lovers, we were friends, and I stupidly told him that I was *playing the field*. He's dropped hints before but never asked me outright if I'm seeing anyone else. He's never come right out and said that he wants us to be exclusive but obviously if I move in with him, we would be.

'Well,' I say, with a light-hearted laugh. 'You'd have to give up all your other girlfriends too.'

Simon gently puts his index-finger under my

chin and tilts my face towards him.

'There are no other girlfriends,' he says, looking at me unsmilingly while staring into my eyes. 'You should know by now how I feel about you. I don't want anyone else.'

Oh God, this is just what I didn't want; I don't want to be tied down and made to pledge undying love but equally, I don't want to stop seeing him. I have a horrible feeling that any minute now he's going to tell me that he loves me and once that's been said, it changes everything.

'So you say.' I smile, in an attempt to lighten the moment and get away from the possibility of him telling me that he loves me. 'But what about your secret admirer? You haven't got rid of her yet, have you?'

He roars with laughter.

'You don't need to worry about her, Lissa. Her feelings are definitely *not* reciprocated.'

'You might say that,' I tease. 'But you haven't blocked her, have you? I think you like her messaging you all the time. I *think*.' I trail my finger down his chest and come to a stop just below his navel. 'That she secretly turns you on.'

He groans and takes hold of my shoulders and flips me over onto my back. We hold each other's gaze for a moment and then he begins to kiss my neck and work his way downwards. I give in to the moment, glad that for now at least, there's no talk of love.

* * *

'You cook the best steak ever,' I say, as I put the last forkful into my mouth.

'I won't argue with that,' Simon says, as he puts a cup of freshly roasted coffee on the table in front of me.

He does too; as well as everything else this man is an excellent cook and he even cleans up after himself. Hugh used to cook but made a huge fuss about it and expected me to scurry around after him like a kitchen porter cleaning up his mess. The resulting meal was never worth the drama or the destroyed kitchen, although of course I had to enthuse about how wonderful it was or else he'd sulk for hours.

I take a sip of the very good coffee that he's made and think back over the day. We've just eaten dinner at the island counter in his vast kitchen and it's nearly nine o'clock. After our morning spent in bed, by the time we'd showered and dressed it was nearly one o'clock and far too late for breakfast. Simon suggested that we go out for lunch to a fabulous new restaurant that he'd discovered in a nearby town. We had a delicious salmon and ginger salad and lingered over a bottle of wine that I mostly drank because Simon was driving, until they practically threw us out so that they could close for the afternoon. We then wandered around the designer shops where Simon insisted on buying me a stunning dress even though I protested that it was far too expensive; although I didn't protest *too* much because obviously, I wanted the dress.

When he suggested that he cook dinner for me tonight, I was going to refuse but then I thought, why not? I've made a point of not staying more than one night at his place but why do I make these rules for myself? One night or two, what does it really matter, it doesn't mean that I'm making any sort of commitment. Also, another reason I thought that I'd break my rule about staying over for two nights is that the thought of going back to miserable Gina's house tonight doesn't appeal at all.

But the more I've thought about it the more I'm coming round to thinking that maybe I should move in with him for a while and see how it goes.

'I got them at that little butcher's shop that's opened in the old town,' he says, taking a sip of coffee, breaking my chain of thought. 'Much better than the supermarket stuff, even Waitrose doesn't come close.'

'It was fabulous,' I say. 'Much better than my cooking.' It tasted just like any other steak to me but I'm not going to spoil it for him by telling him so.

'I could cook for you every night if you like,' he says, staring into my eyes.

I look down at the counter top as if I'm thinking about what he's said but I've actually just made my mind up; sod it and sod Gina, I'm going to move in with Simon.

'What do you say? Will you give this poor guy a chance?'

I look up at him and smile; he *is* completely gorgeous so why not give it a whirl. What's the worst that can happen?

'Okay,' I say, quietly.

'Really?' he says in surprise. 'You mean it?'

'Of course I mean it,' I say. 'But let's take things slowly, yeah? I'm not ready for any kind of commitment just yet. My divorce isn't even through.'

'Of course,' he reaches over and takes hold of my hand. 'One day at a time, eh?'

I nod and feel a bit mean; if Gina wasn't practically throwing me out, I wouldn't have taken up his offer. I'll also have to stop seeing my other men friends which is a bit of a blow because I was quite enjoying having more than one man on the go. But I don't need to move in straightaway so that'll give me a chance to see them for a bit longer and say my goodbyes.

'But it won't be for another couple of weeks,' I say. 'Because I have to give Gina notice so she can get another lodger. I can't just leave her in the lurch.'

He looks slightly annoyed although he tries to hide it and I wonder if I'm making a big mistake.

'Just pay her the rent and move in anyway, it's not like it's much money, is it?' he says.

'Well, I would,' I lie, biting my lip. 'But she's been a good friend to me and I don't want to upset her. She's a bit needy, if you know what I mean and I think it would really affect her if I just moved out without any notice.'

'Lissa, you're just too nice, always thinking of others' feelings,' he says, smiling at me. 'I'll just have to wait, I suppose, but in the meantime, I think this calls for a celebration.' He jumps off the stool and walks across the kitchen, opens the wine fridge and pulls out a bottle of *Moet & Chandon*. He brings it over to the countertop and is about to return to get some glasses when his phone bleeps. He picks it up, glances at it and then puts it down again.

'Anything important?' I ask.

'No.' He shakes his head. 'Just one of my needier clients. I won't answer otherwise he'll think it's acceptable to message me on a weekend – which it most definitely isn't.'

'Really?' I tease. 'Are you sure it's not your secret admirer? Are you waiting until you're alone so that you can open it in private and savour her words?'

'No, it's not,' he laughs. 'My stalker has gone radio silent today; usually I get dozens of messages every day. Maybe she's found someone new to pester.'

'How can you be sure it's a woman,' I ask. 'It could be a man.'

Simon laughs. 'No. It's definitely a woman, no man would write slop like that.'

'You think?' I ask, tapping my lip with my finger. 'Although,' I add. 'I think you must like it otherwise you'd block her. You wouldn't have to put up with her pestering you anymore if you blocked her number.'

'I definitely don't like it,' he says. 'And I was going to block her but a policeman friend of mine advised me not to. He said that if the messages turned into actual stalking, I should keep them as evidence in case I need to get a court order. I don't even bother reading them anymore. It's strange to think that it could be someone I know sending them; or at least someone who I've met. My mate says stalkers have usually met their prey at least once even if it's a completely unmemorable meeting.'

'Creepy,' I say, with a shudder.

'It is,' Simon agrees. 'It could be someone I say hello to every morning or even someone who works with me. It does make me look at people a bit more.'

'I bet,' I say. 'Can I see them?'

'See what?' he asks.

'The messages she sends you.'

Simon laughs. 'Why would you want to see them? They're utter crap, declarations of undying love, ridiculously bad love poems and a log of what she's doing every day. As if I care what she's doing.'

'Show me!' I squeal, my interest piqued. 'I want to see them.'

'Okay.' He seems reluctant but after a moments'

hesitation, scrolls through his phone and passes it to me.

I start to read the messages and he's right, they're excruciatingly cringe-making. There are fifteen messages for yesterday alone and I'm bored with reading them already.

'Oh my God, they're so creepy. You should reply and tell her to leave you alone,' I say.

'What? You must be joking. I don't want to encourage whoever it is. My policeman mate said under no circumstances should I reply, not even to tell her to fuck off because she'll view that as being in a relationship and it'll make her even worse. Maybe that's why she haven't sent any today, she's finally got bored after all these months and given up and moved onto someone else.'

I look at Simon and then at the phone and smile mischievously as I press the call button.

'What the hell are you doing?' Simon looks at me in alarm.

'Ringing her,' I laugh. 'I want to know who it is that thinks they can steal my man.'

He makes a lunge for me and I leap off the stool, laughing, and dance across the kitchen out of his reach.

'It's ringing,' I say, in delight as I hold the phone to my ear. 'I'm going to speak to your secret admirer.'

CHAPTER FOURTEEN

Gina

I've done it.

At nine o'clock this morning I telephoned an estate agent and told them that I want to put my house on the market. Someone is coming round this evening at five o'clock to start the process. I asked if they could come before that but they are extremely busy, I was informed. That's got to be a good thing, hasn't it? Because it must mean that people are buying houses.

I did think that maybe I should ring another agent and see if they could send someone round earlier but it seemed like complicating things. The estate agents I've chosen is the one that sold me the house and it seems to have more *for sale* boards around this area than any other so they seemed the best choice. And actually, it doesn't really matter that they're not coming until five because I have an awful lot to get through today.

Although earlier would have been better to make sure that there is no possibility of him bumping into Lissa.

It should be okay because she doesn't usually get home until nearer six and I'll make sure he's definitely gone by then. Anyway, it's none of her business who visits my house so if she asks me who it is I'll just ignore her.

That's if she's speaking to me.

I'm wondering if she's feeling upset with me about having to move out because I haven't seen her since Thursday evening and it's now Monday. I thought she was bound to come home last night as she'd have work this morning but she didn't. I hope she is upset and it's made things very inconvenient for her and she's feeling miserable. No doubt she's staying with one of her many *friends with benefits.*

Perhaps she won't come back at all; that would suit me very well but is unlikely to happen as all of her belongings are here.

Except for her Rolex watch.

Every time I think of that watch my heart starts to race so much that I wonder if I'm going to have a heart attack. It's not that I care that I effectively stole it but that I don't want to get caught. She's going to notice that it's gone but will she think that she lost it elsewhere? I hope so; she has no reason to think that I've taken it and the only thing I can do is to lie and pretend I don't know what she's talking about if she asks me about it. It's not as if I can do anything about it so it's pointless worrying but I can't help it. Every time I think of the watch, I start to imagine her calling the police and them coming to the house and questioning me. I know that I'd crack and tell them about the bailiffs and I'll end up going to prison. I tell myself I'm being melodramatic but there's no denying that it's all perfectly possible and what I deserve for stealing. I always have been a *worst case scenario* sort of person about everything and it's not doing me any good at all.

I need to put thoughts of going to prison from my mind and concentrate so I can sort all of the debts to ensure that the bailiffs don't call on me again. Resolving to think of nothing but sorting out the mess of my debts, I take the latest final demand from each company from my office and take them into the lounge along with a big notebook and my phone charger. I'm going to be making a lot of calls today and I don't want the phone dying on me. To say I'm not looking forward to ringing all of these debtors would be an understatement but I have no choice; I have to face up to it and try to sort it out.

All companies promise that help is available if you've got into financial trouble and to ring them, so that's exactly what I'm doing. I'm going to be honest and tell them that I'm selling my house which will put me in a good position to pay the debt in full once it's sold. I'm praying that this will be enough to prevent them from sending more bailiffs round and throwing me out onto the streets.

I spent yesterday evening in rather a state; my attempt at watching mindless television was an abysmal failure after James's phone call and I'd already sorted the debtors' letters so there was nothing more that I could actually *do* until this morning. In an effort to distract myself I got into the car and drove to the office and started emptying the filing cabinets into boxes ready to bring home. It needed doing so why not just get on with it? I'll be running what's left of my business from home in the future so I need everything at the house.

I made a good start and returned to the office again yesterday and continued with the packing. I never realised how much stuff I had in that office and I ran out of boxes at lunchtime. Luckily B and Q were open so I zoomed down there and bought lots of boxes. I'm going to need them anyway once I sell the house so it's not as if they'll be wasted. The packing and then ferrying the boxes back here was very time-consuming and it was late by the time I'd finished.

Which stopped me from thinking about James too much.

But once I was home there was nothing to distract me from my thoughts so I did something that was extremely stupid but it was the only thing that I could think of to stop myself from going mad.

I drank myself into oblivion.

It was the one thing that I knew would ensure that I slept through the night. After a bottle and a half of wine I collapsed into bed and slept through – or maybe I was unconscious - until the morning. The downside of this, of course, is that I felt like death when I awoke this morning and I had to force myself to get out of bed. I felt dreadful and after nearly vomiting after a drink of water I decided that the best thing for it would be to get it all up. I stood over the toilet and stuck my fingers down my throat and it was truly as horrific as it sounds but I did feel marginally better afterwards. Not the best thing to do when I have a day of speaking to my debtors but I could think of nothing else to dilute the effects of the hangover. The only upside of having a full day of ringing people is that whilst I'm dealing with my debt, I can't dwell on thoughts of James.

I concentrate and pick up the first letter; the biggest and most pressing debt – my mortgage. I take a deep breath and press the numbers on my phone for the financial difficulty phone line.

When I hang up forty-five minutes later, I breathe a huge sigh of relief. As expected, there is no magic answer to my predicament and I will most definitely have to sell up. There was a tiny part of me that hoped there was some other way

JOANNE RYAN

out of the situation but there isn't. The building
society administrator that I spoke to was very
pleasant but also very firm – I will need to sell
my house as quickly as possible. I told her that I
had already arranged for an estate agent to start
the process today and she said that was a good
start. She's put my mortgage into a special process
which I can't even remember the name of but,
in effect, they won't attempt to take the monthly
payment each month but will contact me weekly
to find out how my sale is progressing. There will
be extra interest accruing on the debt for my non-
payment and if they feel that the house sale is not
progressing quickly enough there is the possibility
that they can step in and force me to lower the
price or even repossess the house. She assured me
that this only ever happens as a last resort but
wouldn't divulge how long I have until it becomes
a real possibility.

Realistically, I have to sell my house as soon as
possible so I'll be asking the estate agent to price
it accordingly. I only hope that I won't have to sell
it for less than the price I paid. Tempted though I
am to search the internet for current house prices
in this area, I've stopped myself. It will make
no difference to the outcome so why inflict the
torture on myself? Besides, I don't have the time; I
may have dealt with the building society but I now
have to work my way through the rest of the final
demands.

I plug my mobile phone into the charger and

begin.

∗ ∗ ∗

By the time the estate agent is due to arrive I've managed to ring every single one of my debtors. I feel relieved but exhausted; my head is pounding and I've eaten nothing all day although I have drunk nearly two large bottles of water. I feared that if I stopped to eat, I would lose momentum and be unable to face starting again.

Mostly, the people I have spoken to were pleasant and polite and, in some cases, sympathetic and genuinely sorry that I've found myself in this situation. Strangely, the sympathetic ones were the hardest to deal with; their unexpected kindness nearly moved me to tears and I had to take a deep breath and force myself to carry on. Only one man was very abrupt with me, verging on rudeness. He asked me why I had let myself get into such a situation by buying things that I couldn't afford as if it was something that I'd done on purpose. I didn't answer and eventually he told me what would happen next and what I needed to do. After I'd made the first call, I didn't find it as humiliating as I'd feared; there are many other people who've been in the same situation as I and they've recovered from it so I can, too.

I telephoned the lettings agency and told them that I needed to give immediate notice on the office. They told me that they would take me to court if I broke the terms of my annual contract that states I have to rent for the full twelve months. I replied that they were welcome to do so but would have to get in line with the rest of my debtors. They eventually agreed that they would charge me until the end of the month – which along with my arrears means that I owe them three months' rent.

I have just a few days to collect my remaining possessions from the office and will do that tomorrow. There is only my computer left to bring home and then I can begin contacting and salvaging the clients that haven't yet deserted me.

If I'm very lucky, the house will sell quickly and I can pick up the pieces of my life and start again. If I can at least sell the house for what I paid for it there will be some left over, even accounting for all the extra interest that I'll be paying.

I look out of the lounge window for what seems like the hundredth time just in time to see a blue BMW pull up onto my driveway. I'm relieved to see that the car has no markings on it to betray the fact that it's from an estate agent. I quickly scan the lounge to make sure that I've left no stray letters around and then go out into the hallway and open the front door. A tall, thin man around my own age is standing in front of me with his hand raised to ring the doorbell.

'Miss Moray' he asks, squinting at me through thick-lensed glasses. 'I'm Jeremy English from

Podens Estate Agents.'

'Hello,' I say. 'Come in.'

He steps inside and I close the front door. Jeremy offers his hand to me and I shake it, noting his limp and slightly damp handshake. He's nothing like any of the estate agents that I've ever met; with his untidy hair, black framed glasses and dandruff-dusted crumpled suit he's more like a school teacher than the sharp-eyed estate agent I was expecting.

'Do you mind?' he asks, pulling his mobile phone out of his pocket. 'I find it easier to record as we go.'

'No, that's fine,' I say.

'I do believe.' He looks around the hallway and up the stairs. 'That our agency sold this house only a year ago. Is that right?'

'Eight months ago, actually.' I find myself blushing and suddenly wish that I'd chosen a different agency.

'Excellent!' Jeremy says. 'That makes it much more straightforward. If you wish to go ahead, we can have it on the market by tomorrow.'

'Really?' I ask.

'Oh, yes.' He nods. 'Most definitely. I'll take some internal photographs and we'll pop it straight on. We may come out when the light is better to take some external pictures but if the previous ones are good, we'll use those.'

'Okay, well I'll show you around.'

He beams at me and I feel relieved that he hasn't

asked why I'm selling so soon. As I show him around the house he enthuses about the size and decor in each room as he clicks the camera on his phone and in no time at all we're back downstairs in the lounge, sitting on the sofas.

I look at the clock; five-forty-five. Lissa could be home at any minute.

'So, Miss Moray,' Jeremy says, adjusting his glasses on his nose for the millionth time. 'I can see no problem at all with getting a good price for this house. I would recommend putting it on the market for four-hundred-and-seventy-five thousand pounds with an expectation of achieving between four-fifty-five and four-sixty-five for a quick sale. House prices have rocketed in the last six months; especially for properties such as this.'

Part of me is annoyed that he assumes I want a quick sale but the other part of me is overjoyed; I paid four-hundred-and-thirty thousand-pounds only eight months ago so will make a profit of at least twenty-five thousand pounds. I'll easily have enough left over for a deposit on a flat.

'That sounds acceptable,' I say. 'Is there a contract that I need to sign?'

'Yes, indeed. I assume that Sandra in the office explained our commission charges to you?'

'She did,' I confirm.

'Excellent. I'll have the contract emailed to you first thing in the morning. If you're happy with everything we've discussed we'll have this super house on the market by tomorrow afternoon.'

'That's great,' I say.

He stands up from the sofa and tucks his mobile phone into his pocket.

'I don't think we'll have any trouble at all selling this,' he says. 'Between you and me we already have several clients on our books who are looking for a house just like this.'

I smile at him but my mind is elsewhere and I can't help looking at the clock again. Five-to-six. He needs to go before Lissa gets back.

'Great,' I say, again. 'Let me show you out.'

I get up and go and open the lounge door and step out into the hallway, praying that Lissa doesn't choose that moment to come home.

Jeremy follows behind me and I hurry across the hallway to the front door and open it. Jeremy walks to the door and steps outside into the porch. He turns to say goodbye but I close the front door on him as he's speaking. He needs to get in his car and leave right now; I haven't time to be shaking hands or any of that nonsense, I want him gone before Lissa gets back and even though I look rude, I don't care.

I go back into the lounge and watch through the window as he walks across to his car and stands next to it and fumbles in his pocket for his keys. I silently scream at him to hurry up, but it's too late.

A white Ford Puma pulls up onto the driveway and parks beside him.

It's Lissa.

CHAPTER FIFTEEN

Lissa

Simon and I have had our first row.

Unbelievably, it was over the stupid cow who's been stalking him. When I grabbed his phone and rang his stalker's number, he jumped up and tried to grab the phone from me so I ran across the kitchen and held it up in the air and laughed. The worried look on his face just seemed so hilariously funny.

He didn't laugh.

He stormed towards me with a face like thunder and roughly grabbed my wrist in his huge hand. He glowered down at me for what felt like minutes but was obviously only seconds, before wrenching his mobile from me with his other hand, giving my fingers a good twisting in the process. He held onto my wrist so tightly I thought he was going to snap it and then he suddenly let go and I nearly fell over. I heard the faint sound of a voice picking up the call but Simon cut it off instantly. I looked up at him in shock and he stared down at me with a grim look on his face.

'Don't you ever touch my fucking phone again,' he growled in a most un-Simon like way.

I told him it was just a joke but he ignored me and turned his back and went and sat back down at the island. I followed and sat down on the stool opposite him and repeated that I was sorry but he wouldn't even look at me. Honestly, I could have hit him except that obviously he's much bigger than me so I wouldn't – not with the mood he was in. I really wanted to tell him to get a sense of humour but there was something about the way he was simmering that stopped me.

Because I had the horrible feeling that *he* might hit *me*.

I sat for a few moments without saying anything and then quietly got up and went upstairs to the bedroom and began to pack my things in my overnight case. I looked at the designer bag on the bed containing the beautiful dress that he'd bought me and wondered if I should take that too. Would I look mercenary if I did that or should I leave it and make it look as if I didn't want it? I decided to leave it for now and take my time putting things into the case because I wanted to give him time to calm down and come upstairs and do some grovelling. I didn't have to wait very long – no more than ten minutes – when I heard his footsteps on the stairs. I had a little smile to myself when I heard him and I ran into the ensuite and splashed water onto my face and pinched my cheeks to make it look as if I'd been crying. When I emerged from the bathroom, he was standing in the middle of the bedroom staring at my case on the bed. When he heard me, he looked up at me and he looked absolutely bereft.

I pretended shock at seeing him even though I knew he was there and he did indeed grovel. It wasn't pretty. If I wasn't absolutely desperate for somewhere to stay, he would have been dumped immediately, there and then. Mr Perfect has revealed himself to be not so perfect after all and I did fleetingly think of telling him I wasn't going to move in. I would go back to Mum and Dad's instead, I thought, but then a vision of their incessant nagging gave me a reality check so I didn't say anything.

Fortunately for me, Simon has shown his true colours over something very trivial and I'd be lying if I denied that it made me a little bit afraid of him. He said that he was angry because he didn't want his stalker to get any ideas about his reciprocating her feelings but I don't think that's the reason at all. I think he panicked that I had his phone because he's got something to hide. I don't know exactly what, because he says he's not seeing anyone else but I can spot a guilty conscience a mile away. So, I will be moving in with him but it will definitely only be temporarily – not that I'll tell him that, of course – because if I ever do want a long term relationship it certainly won't be with someone with a hair-trigger temper like his. He's the best of a bad choice; a grotty house-share, my parents, or an expensive flat rental of my own, and that's the only reason I'm moving in with him.

There's a niggling voice at the back of my head that sounds suspiciously like my mother's, warning me to cut and run while I can, because if I had the feeling that he might hit me then he very well might. I'm ignoring it for now but I may revisit my decision later; I have no wish to get stuck in an abusive relationship.

The rest of the weekend was perfect and as if the phone incident had never happened because we never spoke of it again. After he'd finished grovelling, I said that I was going to have a bath as I had an awful headache. I stayed in the bath for nearly an hour and I closed and locked the bathroom door just so he didn't get any ideas about joining me. When I came out of the bathroom, I told him that my headache was much worse – it wasn't – and that I thought I might go straight to bed.

What could he say but agree with me? We went to bed and although I shut my eyes and pretended to be asleep, I wasn't, I was mulling over what I was going to do.

When we woke on Sunday morning, the sun

was shining and the sky was blue and it was the perfect autumn day. I leapt out of bed and went into the bathroom and got showered and dressed and went downstairs. I knew that if I stayed there, we'd end up having sex and I didn't want to; I suppose I wanted to punish him a bit for the previous night. When he got up, we had breakfast and then went out for a long, meandering walk in the huge park near his house which was full of dog-walkers and families enjoying the weather. Simon then took me for dinner at his favourite Italian restaurant and the day was just perfect. He begged me to stay over again until Monday morning so I did because it was stay with him or go home to misery-guts. Luckily, I always pack a spare dress for work in my overnight suitcase so I was well-prepared.

We watched a movie and then went to bed early because we had to get up for work in the morning. But we didn't go straight to sleep. Simon made no secret of the fact that he wanted, and expected, sex, and I duly obliged. Not that it's ever a chore to have sex with him because he's so hot and such a good lover.

But.

The thing is, gorgeous as he is, I didn't really feel like having sex at all.

But I didn't feel I could say *no*.

❋ ❋ ❋

By the time I finish work on Monday I'm more than ready to go home, have a bath, veg out on the sofa and watch mindless drivel on TV. The day hasn't been bad in a work kind of way; the clients that I've visited have been as enthusiastic and pleased with my designs as they always are but my mind has been elsewhere.

I kept thinking back to Simon's explosion of temper, and try as I might to tell myself that I was over-reacting I couldn't *quite* convince myself. My fingers still feel tender from where he twisted them and there's the faintest hint of a bruise circling my wrist. I can't help imagining what would happen if he really lost his temper and actually hit me. He's much bigger than me and the thought of it makes me feel quite sick.

I was scared of him whilst we were in the kitchen and even though he's apologised and promised never to lose his temper again, I feel that something has shifted in our relationship and I'm now thinking that I need to be careful what I say to him. If he can lose it over something so trivial what if he really blew his top?

So I've decided.

I'm not going to move in with him.

I haven't told him yet; I'm going to take the coward's way out and text him the bad news so I don't have to see him again.

But not yet.

I'll give it a few days and then do it. This means that I need to find somewhere else to live and I'll just have to bite the bullet and look for a small flat to rent. Realistically, it'll be for at least six months because that's the shortest lease that anyone will do; it may even have to be a year. It's just too bad, I can't bring myself to move in with Simon because now I have a bad feeling about him. I can't face moving back in with my parents and there's no way I want another house share. It'll be impossible to find a flat to rent by the end of this week, which is what Gina wants, so she'll just have to wait until I'm good and ready. I plan to tell *her* the bad news tonight.

This is all going through my mind as I attempt to pull up onto the driveway of Gina's house. The next-door-neighbour is faffing about and trying to reverse off his driveway so I have to wait for him to get out of the way before I can pull onto the driveway which gives me a good view of Gina' house. I'm surprised to see her at the front door with a man.

The elusive James, I decide, as I study him; so he's not a figment of her imagination after all.

He looks just as I expected him to; crumpled and swotty with untidy hair and specs. In other words, a complete nerd and not someone I would ever consider going out with. She must be desperate. I wonder if they've had an argument because from the look on her face, she can't wait to get rid of him and she practically slams the door in his face as he steps outside. I curse the old fool next door for delaying me because I want to speak to the boyfriend before he gets in his car. I know Gina will absolutely hate this which is why I want to do it. I'm being a bitch but I can't help it; my plans are ruined so why not take it out on her. It's all her fault that I have to rent an expensive flat because she's socially retarded and can't live with a normal person.

When I'm finally able to move I pull up alongside him as he's fumbling in his pocket for his car keys but before I can leap out of my car, he's found them and has opened the door and got into the driver's seat. I get out of the car and lock my car door and then turn and look down through the window and give him my best smile and a little wave. He flushes scarlet and waves limply back. I know that Gina is watching from the lounge window because I'm sure I saw a movement out of the corner of my eye. It's just the sort of sneaky weird thing she would do.

I get my case out of the boot and drag it across the driveway and unlock the front door and let myself into the house. The lounge door is closed and I know that Gina is hiding in there in an attempt to avoid me. I decide that now is the time to tell her that a week's notice just isn't enough to find a new place to live. I'm just about ready for a row with someone so why not make it her. I walk across the hallway and tap on the lounge door but she doesn't answer. I knock again; I'm starting to feel a bit pissed off, what with the Simon situation, so I put my hand on the door handle to open it but she beats me to it and the door opens.

'Yes?' she says, unsmilingly.

'Hi, Gina,' I say, 'Good day? Was that James I just saw leaving?'

Her face flushes and she looks shocked; as if I've caught her out and I wonder if she's annoyed that I saw them having a row. What a pair; they can't even speak to someone normally without going as red as a beetroot.

'Oh, yes,' she says. 'He had to go and see his mother. She's in a home and he goes at the same time every week otherwise she gets confused.'

'Really?' I say. I mean really, is that the best you can come up with and why would I even care when he sees his mother? I want to laugh but manage to stop myself.

'Yes,' she says. 'Look Lissa, I don't mean to be rude but I'm very busy. Was there something that you wanted?'

She is rude and I think she means to be but she won't put me off from saying what I want.

'Well, Gina, the thing is, I know you want me to move out but a week's notice just isn't enough. I'm never going to be able to find somewhere to live in a week.'

She frowns and I can tell she's fuming but trying to hide it.

'I'm sorry, Lissa, but a week's notice is all I'm able to give you. I need you to move out by Friday. Couldn't you stay at your parents while you look for something else?'

'My parents?' I say. 'You must be mad. No way am I going back there. No, I'm sorry, you'll just have to put up with me while I find somewhere. I'll keep out of your way; you and James won't even know that I'm here.'

'No,' Gina says, quietly. 'I'm sorry but you have to leave by Friday. That's all there is to it.'

The situation suddenly strikes me as completely ridiculous and I laugh as I turn away from her and head towards the stairs; I've had enough of this conversation and it's pointless to continue it. She'll just have to lump it. I step onto the first step and turn to look across at her.

'I'm not going anywhere, Gina,' I say, with another laugh, 'Until I'm good and ready.'

She stares at me in shock and the colour drains from her face and I climb the stairs in triumph.

That's her told.

CHAPTER SIXTEEN

Gina

Why did she have to come home at precisely the moment he was leaving? Why couldn't it have been just a few minutes later? I watch through the window as Lissa jumps out of her car; she seems in an almighty hurry and I know it's because she's nosy and wants to find out who the estate agent is.

Luckily, he's already got into his car by this time and I silently urge him to start the car up and go before she has a chance to speak to him. I don't think I could bear the humiliation of her finding out that I have to sell the house. He starts the car up as she closes her car door and I can see the disappointment on Lissa's face. She is such a nosy bitch. She smiles and waves at the estate agent through the car windscreen and I want to hit her. Why does she feel to need to flirt and flaunt herself at every man she sets eyes on? He's not even remotely attractive but she still has to simper and wave and thrust herself at him. Even from here I can see that the poor man has blushed bright red from his neck up to the roots of his hair and obviously can't wait to get away. Lissa has a big, ugly smirk on her face and is obviously enjoying his embarrassment.

Bitch.

I don't usually judge people so harshly but for her I'll make an exception. The fact that I yearned for her friendship when I was a child completely baffles me now; she is shallow and selfish beyond belief. Thank God she'll be gone from my house and my life by the end of the week and I can have some peace again.

I hear the front door opening and closing and the sound of Lissa's heels clip-clopping across the floor and her case being dragged behind her. She doesn't care one bit if her suitcase wheels scrape my wood flooring or her stupid high heels dig holes into it. As I listen to her getting closer, I hate her so much that I can barely breathe.

My fear that she is going to try and engage me in conversation is confirmed when I hear her impatient tap on the lounge door. I'm not going to answer it; if I pretend I'm not here then she'll give up and go away.

She knocks again, more loudly this time, and I

realise that I'm going to have to speak to her to get rid of her. I walk across the room and open the door to find that she has her hand on the door handle on the other side. The damned cheek of the woman; she was going to let herself into *my* lounge. Friday can't come soon enough for me.

'Yes?' I say, without the merest hint of a smile, aware that I'm being rude but not caring in the slightest. She's leaving in five days so who gives a damn.

'Hi, Gina,' she says, with her fake smile. 'Good day? Was that James I just saw leaving?'

I stare at her for a moment wondering what the hell she's talking about before I realise that she's referring to the estate agent. I feel insulted that she thinks my James is a bespectacled and unattractive, scruffy man but quickly realise that she's unwittingly just given me the perfect explanation for who he is.

'Oh, yes,' I lie, feeling my face flush. 'He had to go and see his mother. She's in a home and he goes at the same time every week otherwise she gets confused.' I have no idea why I feel as if I have to explain to her why he's just left and as I finish speaking, I feel like a complete fool. Why didn't I just say it was James and leave it at that? What on earth did I say all that nonsense for?

'Really?' she asks, in a mocking tone and I realise how ridiculous I must have sounded. I decide the only thing for it is to end the conversation as quickly as possible and get rid of her.

'Yes,' I say. 'Look Lissa, I don't mean to be rude but I'm very busy. Was there something that you wanted?'

I can tell by her expression that she's annoyed and not used to being spoken to so bluntly. She thinks that everyone has to speak to her as if she's a princess and be nice to her.

'Well, Gina,' she says, after a moment. 'The thing is, I know you want me to move out but a week's notice just isn't enough. I'm never going to be able to find somewhere to live in a week.' She smiles her fake smile again and I feel my anger rise. Does she think that she just has to smile and simper and she can stay here for as long as she wants? That may work on everyone else but it's not going to work on me and she's leaving on Friday even if I have to throw her out onto the street myself.

'I'm sorry, Lissa,' I say, firmly. 'But a week's notice is all I'm able to give you. I need you to move out by Friday. Couldn't you stay at your parents while you look for something else?'

'My parents?' she says, looking at me aghast. 'You must be mad. No way am I going back there. No, I'm sorry, but you'll just have to put up with me while I find somewhere. I'll keep out of your way; you and James won't even know that I'm here.' She smirks again and I want to slap her face.

'No,' I insist. 'I'm sorry but you have to leave by Friday. That's all there is to it.'

She stares at me for a moment and then laughs and turns and walks towards the stairs, bumping her case along behind her. In that instant a memory stirs and I push it away and try desperately to ignore it.

She starts to walk up the stairs and I breathe a sigh of relief; she's going and I won't have to tolerate her any longer. But she's not done with me yet; she stops on the stairs and turns to look down at me.

'I'm not going anywhere, Gina,' she calls, laughing her tinkling laugh again. 'Until I'm good and ready.'

And as she stares at me with a triumphant look on her face, the phone call from James on Saturday night comes flooding back to me. When I answered the call, he wasn't there. I heard muffled noises and laughter and I told myself that it was a pocket call; that he'd called me by mistake. Because why would he attempt to ring me when he knew I was away and unlikely to have a phone signal? He was in a pub somewhere, I told myself, and the laughter and muffled voices I heard before the call ended were other customers enjoying a night out. I so wanted to believe it that I'd almost succeeded in convincing myself.

Almost.

The laugh that I heard from his phone that played so heavily on my mind wasn't a stranger in a pub. I knew that I'd heard that laugh before but I couldn't think who it was.

But now I know.

It was Lissa.

There is only one person who laughs like that; fake and girlish, contrived and not natural at all.

Lissa.

Lissa has stolen James from me and that's who she's been with all weekend.

The kiss at the gym; it wasn't a peck on the cheek as I tried to make myself believe. She's been having an affair with him and even had the gall to come back here and mock me by asking if the estate agent was my boyfriend. She knows exactly who my boyfriend is because she's seeing him behind my back. How she must have laughed at my pathetic lie; no wonder she sounded so surprised when I lied about him leaving to see his mother. She's not content with stealing James; she wants to belittle and mock and destroy me. She dares to tell me that she has nowhere to go when she's spent the whole of the weekend with James.

My James.

She's not content with stealing my one true love, she's insisting on staying in my house so that she can flaunt their affair in front of me. She won't leave my house even though I've told her she has to go because she wants to torment me.

What next? Will she bring him here and take him to her room and into her bed? She will, I know she will.

My head is reeling and I feel sick; I am heartbroken at James's betrayal and I truly don't know how I'm going to live without him. How could he do this to me and treat me in this way?

Is it not enough that I've lost my house and my business is in tatters? How can life be so cruel?

My head begins to pound and I briefly close my eyes but the vision of James and Lissa together makes me open them again. My legs feel as if they've turned to jelly and I put a hand out to the doorframe to steady myself.

I must stay calm.

I look at the stairs and watch as Lissa slowly climbs the stairs, the case bumping behind her. Each step she takes is mocking me, each bump of her case taunting and laughing at me. A feeling of hatred so strong washes over me that I have to force myself to close the lounge door and lean against it so that I no longer have to look at her. If I have to look at her for one moment longer, I won't be responsible for my actions.

I want to kill her.

CHAPTER
SEVENTEEN

Lissa

So much for my plan to text Simon to tell him I'm not moving in with him or seeing him again.

Somehow, it's all turned to shit.

When I left him on Monday morning to go to work, I never gave him the slightest hint that we were over. I deliberately didn't give him any indication at all because I intended dumping him by text and letting him down gently. I didn't want to have to talk to him about it or explain myself or give him any opportunity to lose his temper.

Out of the blue on Tuesday afternoon he texted me and asked what I was doing that evening. He *never* normally texts me on a Tuesday and I honestly didn't think that I'd hear from him until at least Thursday because he has a very time-consuming job. I can only think that maybe I'm not such a good actress as I think I am and he somehow suspected that I'd gone off him. His text said that he'd cook dinner for me if I wanted to go over to his place that evening.

No thanks, I thought, definitely not.

He may be hot, rich and good in bed but I'm a little bit afraid of him now and that's not good.

So I took the plunge and texted that I didn't want to see him again. Obviously, I didn't tell him the real reason but said that I thought it best if I didn't see him for a while as I was going through a very messy divorce. I said that I was sorry to mess him around but I needed to be on my own while I untangled myself from Hugh. I thought I'd put it rather nicely; I thanked him for the wonderful times we'd had together and said something vague about maybe seeing him in the future and that I hoped we could be friends.

As I expected he didn't like getting dumped one little bit and proceeded to blow up my phone for the rest of the day.

Why, why, why? He kept asking.

I reiterated what I'd said in my first text and then just ignored his texts after the first few but by this morning – Wednesday – it was getting ridiculous. At first, he was begging me to reconsider but eventually, as I suspected would happen, his texts turned nasty. He started calling me a gold-digger and other horrible names so I had to resort to blocking him.

I told Ffion, the secretary that I share with the other designer, not to put calls through from Simon Kingley under any circumstances. I had no desire to get caught on the phone to him whilst under the scrutiny of my work colleagues.

I thought that I'd covered all bases until she put a call through to me and it turned out to be Simon – I'd stupidly forgotten that although everyone calls him Simon, that's not his actual name. I never took much notice of his real name but vaguely remembered him saying that he was known by his second name to avoid confusion as his first name was the same as his father's. I must have known on some level that his initials were JS Kingley but honestly, why would I even remember that? It wasn't as if I was some pleb in the accounts department sending him the invoices for the interior design on his house.

Which is why when Ffion put a call from Jim through to me, I never gave Simon a thought. He never even entered my head. I didn't know who was on the line and assumed it was a recommendation from another client. Jim is an older person's name so I never connected it with Simon at all. When I picked up the call he spoke very quietly and asked if he was speaking to Lissa.

I didn't even realise it was him.

I asked him who he was and he answered, *don't you know? How many other men are you fucking, whore?*

My stomach flipped over and I slammed down the phone with shaking hands. It was the way he said it; he really frightened me and I wondered quite what I'd let myself in for by going out with him. I sat and thought about it for a while and then decided that the best thing I could do was ignore him; if you don't give something air it will eventually die. Besides which he must have loads of women after him who'll be only too happy to take my place. I think the reason that he's so pissed off is that I finished with *him* and not the other way around.

I'm sure that if I ignore him, he'll soon get bored and go away.

✻ ✻ ✻

I pull up outside the house and see that it's in darkness; this means that Gina's not in. I haven't seen her since Monday so she's either working late or avoiding me.

Either will do so that I don't have to see the miserable cow.

I let myself in the front door and go around putting the downstairs hallway and kitchen lights on. I don't quite know why.

Yes, I do.

The phone call from Simon has put me on edge because darkness doesn't normally bother me in the slightest. I check that the front door is locked and then go straight upstairs and get changed into my comfortable joggers and baggy top.

Before the horrible phone call from Simon, I was going to see one of my other men friends but I've gone off the idea now. Simon's put me off men for a while so I think I'll have some me time and catch up with some old girlfriends. I'm not feeling quite so free and single now, more alone and slightly scared.

For the first time since I left Hugh I wonder if I've done the right thing; my old life wasn't so terrible, was it? I was never scared when I was with Hugh; a bit bored maybe but never afraid. He wasn't that bad and when we first got married, we had lots of fun. Even when the boredom set in, we still had a very good lifestyle so I wonder if I might have been a bit hasty. It suddenly strikes me that maybe it's not too late to change my mind because we're not actually divorced yet; there's still time for a rethink.

Unless his new girlfriend has really got her hooks into him.

I need to properly think about things; Simon turning nasty has rattled me but I don't want to do anything rash that I'm going regret.

I throw my work clothes on the floor and empty the laundry basket onto the floor next to it and sort through until I have a sufficient load to put in the washing machine. Before taking it downstairs I search through my chest of drawers and dressing table yet again for my watch but don't find it.

I knew that I wouldn't.

Did I leave it at Simon's house?

I'm certain that I didn't because I *never* wear it to work and I stayed at Simon's from Thursday night until Monday morning. I remember leaving it here on the chest of drawers where I always put it and now it's not there.

Has Gina taken it?

She's miserable and socially retarded but that doesn't make her a thief, does it? I honestly can't imagine her stealing it because she has pots of money and could easily buy herself a Rolex if she wanted to; she could probably afford to buy several.

But that doesn't alter the fact that my watch is missing and it's worth a lot of money. Hugh bought it for me on our fifth wedding anniversary and I remember how delighted I was when he gave it to me. It was a complete surprise and I was shocked at how generous he was; his job wasn't so well paid then and he'd saved up for months so he could buy it. He *was* very generous and maybe I'd forgotten that when I was so busy finding fault with him. As I gather up the dirty washing from the floor, I start to feel a little sad at how I've treated him and wonder if I've been a bit selfish.

But that won't help find my watch.

I more or less took my bedroom and lounge apart on Monday night when I realised it was missing so I know that it's not here; it's most definitely gone.

I used to have the watch insured against loss

or theft but I don't now; once I left Hugh all that lapsed as it was tied to the house. Maybe I could claim against the policy and pretend that Hugh and I are still living together. I could tell the insurance company that I lost it, which isn't a lie. It would also be a good excuse to get in contact with Hugh again; if we were to meet, I could see whether I still have feelings for him and see how the land lies.

But it isn't right that I have to lie because someone has stolen my watch and logically, either Gina took it as she's the only other person living here or her cleaner who comes in every week did. Her cleaner doesn't clean my rooms but that doesn't mean she didn't take my watch.

I should confront Gina about it; that watch isn't lost, it's been stolen. Unless she has stolen it; she *could* be a thief because how much do I really know about her?

A memory from my childhood suddenly pops up; Gina disappeared half-way through my first school term and didn't reappear until after the Christmas holidays. I wasn't particularly interested in Gina but I do remember at breakfast one morning asking my parents what was wrong with Gina. Mum replied that she was ill and in hospital but when I questioned her further, she didn't know exactly what was wrong with her. Mum got quite annoyed with me for repeatedly asking. Dad carried on reading his newspaper but I remember thinking at the time that there was something they weren't telling me. They were usually very open with me and I could tell something was amiss.

When Gina returned to school in the January there were all sorts of rumours flying around; she'd had her appendix out, she'd been raped and had a baby, she'd been run over by a car; all sorts of nonsense that twelve-year-olds make up but I never did find out the real reason. A few days after her return she was old news because no one was really interested in her and it was quickly forgotten about.

Perhaps I'll visit Mum and Dad and ask them; they obviously knew the real reason but it wasn't suitable for my ears then but I'm sure it is now.

Maybe she'd been caught stealing; *maybe* she's a kleptomaniac.

I'm being ridiculous, I know, but someone has stolen my watch and there are only two suspects and she's one of them.

I gather up the pile of dirty washing and go downstairs and into the utility room. I load the washing machine and put the powder and fabric conditioner in and set it going. I go back into the kitchen and pull open the fridge to see what I can cook for dinner. I take out the pack of chicken that I bought last week and check the date; two days past it's sell by date. I throw it into the waste bin and contemplate scrambled eggs on toast. That's about all there is to eat; I only hope there's some bread in the cupboard.

I crack three eggs into a bowl and whisk them up with a fork. There's a fresh loaf of bread in the cupboard which is Gina's because I haven't bought any. I help myself to a couple of slices and pop them in the toaster. Technically it's stealing but what's two slices of bread compared to a Rolex watch?

The sound of the front door opening makes me jump; Simon has really done a number on me and I curse him for making me so nervous. I pop my head around the kitchen door and see Gina hanging up her coat and slipping her shoes off. She never wears her shoes in the house; not even to cross the hall to the kitchen. I feel a flash of annoyance at her over-the-top fastidiousness. Every time I come into the house, I can see the irritation on her face when I fail to remove my shoes before stepping off the doormat; which is why, of course, I do it.

'Hi, Gina,' I call, in the pleasantest voice I can manage.

She totally ignores me and heads towards the lounge.

The annoyance I felt at the sight of her quickly turns to anger. How dare she ignore me; if she thinks she can avoid me by shutting herself in the lounge she can think again.

'Gina,' I say more loudly, stepping out into the hallway. 'I want to speak to you.'

She stops in her tracks and slowly turns her head to look at me.

'My watch is missing,' I say.

'What?' She frowns.

'My watch is missing,' I repeat.

'And what,' she asks, putting her hand on the lounge door handle. 'Has that got to do with me?'

'Because it's a very expensive Rolex. It was in my bedroom and now it's not.'

'Maybe you left it somewhere.'

'I didn't. It was in my room.'

'Maybe,' she says, with a sneer. 'You left it in one of your lovers' beds.'

I stare at her and think how much I dislike her; how fucking weird she is and the trouble she's causing by making me move out. I choose my next words carefully and pick them to deliberately hurt her.

'I haven't left it anywhere,' I say, walking towards her until my face is only inches from hers.

'I think,' I say, staring at her. 'That you've stolen it.'

CHAPTER EIGHTEEN

Gina

I thought she'd be upstairs in her rooms by now; I wasn't expecting her to be in the kitchen.

I wasn't expecting her to confront me about the watch.

I stayed at the office all day but it wasn't as if I was even doing anything. I'd already brought all the files home and all that was left there were my PC and printer. I locked the outside door of the office so that no one could get in and if anyone tried, they'd think that I was closed.

Which of course, I am. Permanently.

Not that anyone tried to get in; how can I have not noticed that I was receiving hardly any telephone calls when I was at work? Although as

Susie informed me, I wasn't even there very much and I wasn't visiting clients either, so where was I?

I can't remember where I was but I think I must have been like this for a while.

I remember it was like this once before; it's *the thing we never talk about* happening again. I'm unravelling.

When Lissa spoke to me I ignored her; I wanted to escape into the lounge and shut the door but she wouldn't let me. I tried to tell her that I didn't know what she was talking about but she wouldn't shut up. I lost my temper a little and told her that perhaps she'd left it in one of her lovers' beds and I could see that she was shocked that I'd said it. I thought then, that she would leave me alone.

But she didn't.

She came out of the kitchen and walked over to me and got so close to me that I could smell the coffee on her breath. I stared at her perfect face and I hated her more than I've ever hated anyone in my whole life and I include my mother and father in that. All I could think about was her and James laughing and making fun of me the way she made fun of me all those years ago at school. I imagined her in his arms and in his bed and I wanted to scratch her baby blue eyes until they bled. How I yearned to put my hands around her throat and squeeze and squeeze and squeeze until there was no breath left in her body.

But I didn't.

But only because I think she might be stronger

than me.

I told her that she was being ridiculous but she wouldn't have it. She stormed back into the kitchen and said that unless I pay her for it or produce the watch, she's going to call the police first thing in the morning and let them deal with it.

That will be the end of me if she calls the police in. The bailiff's visit and all of the money that I owe will be revealed for the whole world to see and my humiliation will be laid bare. It'll be in the newspapers and everyone will know what I've done.

I can't bear it.

I'll be accused and found guilty of theft and I'll never be able to run my business again. Everything that I've worked for will be gone as well as James; my house, my business, everything.

I shut the lounge door and leaned against it stop her getting in but she didn't even try; she'd said all she needed to say. I was under no illusion that she wouldn't follow through on her threat.

When I eventually open the door after an hour the kitchen light is off and the hallway is in darkness and she's gone. I walk over to the bottom of the stairs in the darkness and I can see the light shining from underneath her lounge door so I know that she's still upstairs.

I return to the lounge and pull the curtains closed against the darkness and put the lamps on. I sit down and try to think what to do. Is there still hope for me? Is there still time to stop everything from unravelling and salvage what's left of my life? There must be a way. Given time, I will get over the heartbreak of James even though it doesn't seem possible at the moment, I have to remind myself that he doesn't deserve me for treating me so badly even though Lissa bewitched him.

I can see clearly that everything that's gone wrong in my life is because of Lissa; James and I were happy until she came along and stole him. My business was thriving and turning a good profit before I got distracted by her behaviour and took my eye of the ball.

It's all *her* fault.

I sit immobile and close my eyes while my thoughts whirl around; time passes but I have no idea how long I've been sitting like this when I finally open my eyes.

I know what I have to do; there is only one way out of this mess.

I get up from the sofa and go out into the hallway and put the light on. I slip my feet into the shoes that I'd left on the front door mat and go into the kitchen and put the light on in there. I pause for a moment and take a deep breath; once I have done this there is no going back.

It's okay.

I quickly type a message on my mobile phone but I don't send it. That will be for after.

I lean on the counter top and inspect the selection of knives in the wooden knife block. They were an extremely expensive set and are supposed to stay sharp for a lifetime without the need for sharpening. I don't see how that's possible but it doesn't matter; I've hardly used them. They're mostly for show as I rarely entertain.

No, that's not right.

I never entertain.

Because I have no friends.

I push the thought away and refuse to think about it; now is not the time for dwelling on irrelevant trivia. I take hold of the handle and pull out the largest knife from the block. The blade is long and slender and lethal looking; I think it's for carving joints of meat.

Too big, I think.

I pull out each knife in turn and inspect them thoroughly before finally deciding on the medium-sized blade. I'm sure that I've never used this knife; I touch the blade gently with the pad of my thumb and wince as it immediately draws blood. The knife is a manageable size and I feel the weight of it in my hand as I study it.

It will do.

I grasp the handle firmly in my hand and take a deep breath.

It's time.

❊ ❊ ❊

I hear the sound of footsteps running down the stairs and know that my text message to Lissa has worked; if it hadn't, I would have gone upstairs to her but it's better that she comes to me.

'Oh my God!' Lissa stops abruptly in the kitchen doorway and stares at me in shock.

'What have you done?' she shrieks, and I see the horror on her face.

I stare up at her from my position on the floor; I'm kneeling and am bent over, clutching my arms to my body. The splatters of scarlet blood around me are in stark contrast to the stone coloured floor tiles and the tea-towels wrapped around each wrist are rapidly growing red where the blood is seeping through.

Lissa is looking at me in disbelief and I see her eyes widen as she takes in the blood on the floor. She makes a strange whimpering noise and her breathing is rapid; she's panicked and like most people in an emergency situation, unsure what to do.

'Why? Why have you done it?' Lissa shrieks at me. 'Nothing's that bad. You didn't need to do that.'

'I'm sorry,' I say, pathetically, repeating the words that I sent in my text to her a few minutes ago. 'I couldn't think straight.'

'Never mind that now.' Lissa opens a kitchen drawer and roughly pulls out two more tea towels, sending the towels below tumbling to the floor. 'Let me tie these around your wrists and then I'll take you to hospital. It'll be quicker than calling an ambulance.'

I start to unwrap the bloodied towels from my

wrists.

'No!' she shouts. 'Leave them! I'll put these over them.'

She kneels down and I sit mutely while she wraps a tea towel over each wrist and ties them as tightly as possible.

'Can you walk?' she asks, as she straightens up.

'I don't know,' I say. 'I feel very weak.'

She bends down and puts her hands around my waist and helps me to stand upright.

'Can you stand there while I go and get my car keys?' she asks.

I nod and sway slightly and put a hand out to the kitchen counter to steady myself.

'Oh, God.' She pulls a chair out from under the table and takes hold of my shoulders and lowers me onto it.

'I'll be two minutes,' she says. 'Just hang on.' She runs from the kitchen and I hear the sound of her running up the stairs and in what seems like seconds she is back.

'Right. Are you okay to walk?' she asks, as she comes back into the kitchen. Her face is pale and her lips slack and she looks like she wants to cry. I suddenly want to laugh out loud but manage to stop myself; I think I might be slightly hysterical so I nod and answer her question without speaking. She comes over to me and puts her arm around my waist and guides me towards the front door as if I've forgotten where it is. She opens the door and pushes me outside and the wind and rain that started this evening batter us as we stand there while she closes and locks the door. She fumbles with the keys and I see that her hands are shaking so badly that she has trouble getting the key in the lock.

She presses the button on her car key to unlock the car door and then helps me into the passenger seat as if I'm an invalid. I hold my hands in front of me as she leans across me and buckles me into the seat belt. I sit mutely while she gets in and starts the car up.

'There's a shortcut,' I say, quietly.

'What?' she looks over her shoulder and reverses the car at speed off the driveway. She pulls onto the road and we drive rapidly towards the main road.

'To the hospital,' I say. 'I know a shortcut.'

'Okay,' she says. 'Do you feel up to giving me directions because I'm not sure of the way from your house.'

'Yes,' I say. 'I'm feeling a bit faint but I'm sure I'll be okay.'

She looks at me in alarm and we veer slightly as she takes her eyes off the road.

'I'll be fine,' I say, not sounding fine at all.

Lissa puts her foot down on the accelerator and we zoom along the road. When we get to the junction, I direct her onto the main road and we hurtle along through the driving rain. Visibility is poor with the rain and the darkness and Lissa leans towards the windscreen and squints into the gloom. We're breaking the speed limit and I can feel Lissa's panic in the air. We cross two more roundabouts and then take the road that runs through the outskirts of the town. We see few other cars and the road we are on has no street lights to guide us. This road doesn't lead to the hospital at all, it meanders through the countryside passing through small villages and hamlets.

'You okay?' Lissa asks. She sounds breathless and frightened and I wonder if she's blaming herself.

She should.

'I'm okay.' I stare out of the window; there are no signs of houses and I know that this part of the road stretches for several miles before passing through a small hamlet. The road is tree-lined which makes it even darker and I think that now is the right time.

'I'm sorry,' I say.

'You don't have to keep saying sorry,' Lissa says.

'Oh, but I do,' I say, as I lean towards her and firmly press her seatbelt button. Her seatbelt releases and flies across her body and she turns and looks at me in surprise. Before she has a chance to speak, I grab the steering wheel with both hands and turn it sharply towards the side of the road.

As we veer towards the trunk of a large tree my last thought is that whilst my seatbelt might save me, Lissa's definitely won't save her.

CHAPTER NINETEEN

Lissa

The police have some more questions for me.

The ward sister approached me and asked if I felt up to speaking to them again. I don't really feel up to it; I just want to go to sleep and wake up and have everything back to how it used to be but I know that's not going to happen. I told her yes, that I'd see them, because I want to get it over with.

And I also have some questions of my own to ask them now that I'm more with it. I can't remember exactly how long ago it was that I last spoke to them because the days have all merged together. I concentrate and try to think but can't remember if it was yesterday or the day before. My head seems to hurt more when I try to concentrate and I wonder why I bother; what does it matter when I spoke to them?

It doesn't.

I gently touch the dressing taped to the side of my face and wonder when the doctors will decide to let me see what's underneath. I remember very little about the accident after Gina undid my seatbelt; I remember the tree heading towards us and then thankfully, nothing, until I woke up in this bed. I hope I never remember; who wants to relive the pain of crashing through a windscreen into a tree?

I fear that my face is ruined; each time I ask the doctor how it's healing they say that I have to be patient and that only time will tell.

But I've noticed the way their eyes won't meet mine; I know that I'm going to be scarred for life because no one can go through a car windscreen and hit a tree without having life-long scars. The doctors say that because I turned my head away from the windscreen just before we hit the tree only one side of my face was badly damaged. They assure me that should it not heal well there is always the possibility of plastic surgery. This tells me that it won't heal well and they're trying to prepare me for it without actually saying the words.

Aside from my facial injuries one arm is broken and my other wrist is broken so badly that they had to operate and pin it back together. My entire body is black and blue with bruises but fortunately, no more broken bones.

The doctors and paramedics agree that I'm lucky to be alive.

I don't feel lucky.

I know that my broken bones will heal and the bruises will fade but what about my face? It will never be perfect again even if I'm able to have plastic surgery.

'Miss Hewson?'

I turn my head slightly and wince with pain. The man and woman standing at the side of the bed are the police officers who visited me before. They don't wear police uniforms but there's something about them that tells me I would know they were police without them needing to tell me.

'Hello,' I say, thinking how foolish of them to ask as who else would I be?

'Detective Inspector Rankin and my colleague Detective Constable Larson. We spoke earlier in the week? Do you feel up to answering a few more questions?'

I tell them that I am but I wonder what else it is that they need to know. I have already told them everything that happened that night, from the moment that I arrived home from work. They would tell me nothing about Gina, who must surely be dead because they told me that the road was so quiet that evening that it was at least an hour before the car was found. I'm not a doctor but I'm sure she would have bled to death from her slit wrists long before we were found.

Accident. It wasn't an accident; that mad bitch decided to kill herself and take me with her.

I watch as DI Rankin pulls two chairs to the side of the bed whilst DC Larson grabs the curtain and swishes it around the bed. I want to tell him not to bother because I have nothing to hide from the other patients in this ward.

I've done nothing wrong.

'So, Miss Hewson, we have a bit of an update for you and you'll be pleased to know that you're not going to be charged with dangerous driving.'

I stare at him and wonder if I'm hearing things.

'What are you talking about?' I croak. 'I told you that she pulled the steering wheel out of my hands, why would I be charged with anything? I'm the victim here; I nearly died thanks to her.'

DI Rankin smiles condescendingly and I glance at DC Larson and she gives me the merest hint of a smile and rolls her eyes. I remember then what a pedantic arse the DI is; his questioning of me last time took far longer than necessary and I think he was rather enjoying himself.

'So.' DI Rankin turns to me, 'Having spoken to Gina Moray, she has....'

'She's alive?' I shout, interrupting him.

'Oh, yes,' he says. 'Very much so, she's confirmed that the events that led to the accident were exactly as you told us. There will be no charges against you, as DC Larson has so kindly informed you, although you may be required at a later date to attend court as a witness.'

'But she slit her wrists!' I protest.

DI Rankin shakes his head from side to side with a condescending smile and if I was able, I'd leap off the bed and punch him on his big fat, nose. I wonder how DC Larson stomachs working with him.

'No, Miss Hewson, she didn't slit her wrists although she pretended to you that she had,' he says, slowly. 'She made superficial cuts on her fingers which bled profusely, leading you to believe that she was in danger of imminent death so that you would take her to the hospital. Due to the fact that she was wearing her seatbelt, aside from being badly bruised her injuries were minimal.'

Superficial cuts. Minimal injuries. I can't believe it, I thought she would have bled to death by the time we were found. The bitch.

'Why?' I ask, but as I utter the word I already know.

'Because she believed that you were having a relationship with her boyfriend.'

'James?' Her James was Simon; she met him once so never even knew that he's known by his second name of Simon.

'Yes, Mr Kingley. Although having spoken to Mr Kingley it appears that Miss Moray was in fact not having a relationship with him at all; or rather in her mind she was but in reality, she wasn't.'

I close my eyes and try to make sense of it. It was her.

'She was stalking him,' I say. 'Sending text messages of undying love.'

'That is correct,' DI Rankin drones. 'Not actual stalking as no threats were made but she did believe that he was cheating on her with you. She thought that you had been seeing him to deliberately hurt her. She mentioned something about a phone call that was made from Mr Kingley's mobile phone where you taunted her but, truthfully, we were unable to make sense of what she was saying and had to terminate our interview with her.'

The day I dialled the number on Simon's phone, the day he wrenched the phone from my fingers and showed his true colours. It was her; she was the woman who answered the phone.

'You'll be charging her with attempted murder?' I ask.

DI Rankin clears his throat before replying.

'Possibly at some point in the future. For now, she's medically unfit to stand trial and whether she's charged once she's received treatment will be for the CPS to decide. For the foreseeable future she's being detained in a secure facility where she's receiving treatment.'

'Treatment!' I shout, making DI Rankin's eyes widen. 'What about me? What about my ruined life? She tried to kill me and scarred me for life and I didn't even DO anything.'

'Miss Hewson, I appreciate....' DI Rankin starts to say.

'No, you don't,' I scream at him. 'You don't appreciate anything. She's ruined my life and you're letting her get away with it.'

* * *

The ward sister gave me something to calm me down after she'd ushered the police out of the ward. I had the impression that my fellow patients were embarrassed at my outburst. But I don't care.

I feel calmer now and quite sleepy but I'm still mad as hell at that mad bitch Gina.

She's got away with trying to kill me and ruined my life.

It's not fair; just because she's completely bat-shit crazy it shouldn't mean that she gets away scot-free. There's also my watch; she obviously took it out of my room. I want it back. The next time I see the police I'm going to tell them about it and they can prosecute her for theft, too, when she eventually comes out of the nut house. These thoughts are whirling around in my head and I drift off into a fitful sleep, only waking when the sound of voices penetrates my dreams. I open my eyes and slowly turn my head around to look in the direction of the noise. Mum and Dad are standing at the entrance to the ward; Mum has a shopping-bag with her and I guess it's stuffed with chocolates and carbohydrates to tempt me to eat. Mum doesn't seem to understand that the last thing I want to do is eat and that a bar of chocolate is not going to fix things.

They're with the ward sister and listening intently to her; she's no doubt filling them in on the police visit. They look as if they're about to leave when Mum notices me looking in their direction. She nudges Dad and they both look over and smile and make their way towards my bed in the same way that they've done every day since I woke up here.

'Hi, darling,' Mum trills in her *let's be jolly and pretend everything's going to be fine* voice.

Dad doesn't speak but comes around the bed and kisses me on the forehead.

'How are you feeling?' Mum asks, as she unloads grapes and a box of chocolates onto the bedside cupboard. She arranges it neatly, squaring the box with the cupboard corners and then places a plastic case with three cupcakes in it on top of the chocolates.

'Okay,' I mumble.

'Your favourites, darling,' she says, nodding at the cupcakes as she sits down.

'Thanks, Mum.' I'll give them to my neighbour in the next bed when they've left.

'I hear the police have been to see you,' Dad says, keen to get the latest update.

I fill them in on the news that Gina is alive and in a secure nut house and they're as shocked as I am. Mum keeps saying it's *so unfair* and I wish she'd just shut up and they'd both go home and leave me to wallow in self-pity. What I really want to know is when I'm going to see Hugh. I told Mum and Dad not to let him visit when I first woke up because I didn't want him to see me looking such a mess but now, I've changed my mind. The doctors have informed me that my injuries are going to take time to heal so I think it's pointless to wait.

Hugh isn't shallow and I know that he loves me for who I am. He's not at all squeamish because he loves to watch all of the medical documentaries on TV so my bruises and broken bones won't bother him at all. Anyway, don't the marriage vows say *in sickness and in health*? They do – and it's not as if I'm not going to get better, I am.

I've had time to do a lot of thinking since I've been here and I've decided that maybe, just maybe, I could reconsider the *not having a baby* thing.

If the whole horrific experience has taught me anything it's that our marriage is worth saving. I now realise that I made the worst decision of my life when I left Hugh. I don't honestly know what I was thinking and I wonder if it was some sort of early mid-life crisis. I think I panicked about the whole *having a baby* issue when what I should have done was sit down and think about it rationally. I know now that I just want to be back with Hugh in our old home with our old life.

'Have you spoken to Hugh?' I ask Mum.

'Yes,' she says.

'And?' I demand.

'He's going to visit this afternoon. He was so shocked about what's happened to you, he couldn't quite believe it,' Mum says. 'We told him that you're going to be fine and not to worry too much because your injuries aren't life-threatening or life-changing.'

Well thanks for that, Mum. I wanted him to be desperately grateful for the fact that I'm still alive and not under the illusion that I've got a few cuts and bruises. I wanted to be the brave heroine who's not making a fuss. Although on the other hand him not knowing how bad I am could be a good thing; he'll be shocked when he sees the state of me and knowing Hugh he'll go into super-protective mode and smother me with love and attention.

I zone out as Mum prattles on about the next-door neighbour and other trivia and wonder if there is some way I can get one of the nurses to wash my hair before this afternoon. It's not been washed since I've been here and although I can't see it, I'm sure it must look like rats' tails as I normally wash it every day.

As soon as Mum and Dad have gone, I'll ask.

Most people are happy to do as I ask.

* * *

The young nurse assigned to me said she'll wash my hair tomorrow but there was no chance she could do it today as the ward is very busy and they're a staff member down. I was disappointed but then thought that there's no point in sulking about it because I'm completely at their mercy.

Every time the ward door opens, I look to see if it's Hugh and each time I'm disappointed. In the end he doesn't arrive until nearly three o'clock and I'd almost given up. He stops and asks the nurse at the desk which bed is mine. As I watch him coming towards me, I realise that I'd forgotten how good looking he is. Much better looking than Simon; why did I ever think that life on my own would be better than living with Hugh?

'Lissa.' Hugh stands by the side of the bed and looks down at me. 'Jesus, what happened to you?'

'Hugh, it's so good to see you.' As I stretch my lips into a smile, I feel the weight of the dressing on one side of my face and tears spring to my eyes.

'It's not as bad as it looks,' I say. Yes it is, it's worse.

He pulls a chair round from the end of the bed and places it close to me and sits down.

'Two broken arms, bloody hell,' he says.

I don't correct him.

'How long do you think you'll be in here?' he asks.

'Another few days and then I can go home as long as there's someone to look after me.'

He nods.

'I don't suppose you'll be able to do much with those.' He nods at my arms; both are encased in plaster although I should be able to use my hands once the swelling has gone down.

'What actually happened?' he asks. 'Your mum said something about the friend of yours you were living with attempting suicide, but I couldn't really make sense of it.'

'I can't either,' I say. 'She wasn't really a friend; I was just renting a room in her house. She has serious mental health problems and somehow, I got caught up in it. I honestly thought that she'd tried to kill herself. I was taking her to hospital when she went completely mad and tried to kill us both.' I watch him as I speak and wonder exactly what Mum told him. She doesn't know the full story as I tried to keep my relationship with Simon out of the version I told her. I said he was a client – which wasn't a lie – because I knew I'd never hear the end of it if she knew the truth.

'Christ, what a nightmare. I'm so sorry this has happened to you. There's no way you'll be going back to live there, then?'

I shake my head and then remember that I shouldn't because it hurts.

'I can go and pick your stuff up for you, if you like,' Hugh offers.

I look at him and a warm feeling washes over me and I suddenly feel happier and more relaxed. Everything is going to be fine; I can move back in with Hugh and it'll be like it used to be before this nightmare began.

'Thank you,' I say. 'That would be wonderful. Mum and Dad have the keys.'

'Okay, I'll get that sorted,' Hugh says, with a smile.

'Hugh,' I say, quietly. 'The only good thing to

come out of all this horror that I've been through is that it's made me realise what's important.'

We stare at each other and the air feels charged with promise.

'Do you think,' I continue. 'That we could try again? Pretend that these last few, hideous months never happened?'

He leans closer to me and I wait for him to kiss me.

'Lissa,' he says, in almost a whisper. 'Just so you know. We're done. Over. Finished. Dead.'

I gawp at him in disbelief, unable to comprehend what he's just said.

'I'm afraid you don't get to treat me like shit and then expect me to take you back for more of the same,' he continues. 'I've moved on, I suggest you do, too.'

I stare dumbly at him and he stares right back at me unflinchingly and I know that he means every single word.

'Anyway,' he says, in a louder voice, looking at his watch and standing up. 'I've got to go. I've got a viewing booked for half-four and I don't want to be late.'

'A viewing?' I whisper.

'Yeah, it's their second one so fingers crossed they'll buy the house and then we can get things moving.' He smiles and holds his crossed fingers up in the air.

I stare at him dumbly. I had no idea the house – our house – was up for sale.

'Have a good life, Lissa.' He smirks. 'And don't fret about your stuff. I'll drop it all off at your parents' house.'

CHAPTER TWENTY

Gina's mother

'She won't see you. I'm sorry,' Doctor Harper says, as he comes into the room and closes the door behind him. He looks embarrassed.

I'm not surprised, nor even disappointed. I came here out of duty and once I've told him what he needs to know I'll leave. Or he may already know; I have no idea what sort of medical records are kept after twenty years but I'll soon find out.

'That's quite alright,' I say. 'I didn't think she would. I came here because I thought you might need to know about Georgina's history. I have copies of the notes for her treatment when she was a child. You may already have them, of course.'

'Please, sit down Mrs Richardson,' Doctor

Harper says, dropping into his chair and indicating the threadbare chair in front of his desk.

I sit down and perch on the edge of the seat. I put the envelope containing Georgina's records onto the desk and push it towards him.

Doctor Harper sits in a swivel chair reclined so far back that it looks in danger of tipping over. He makes no move to look at the contents of the envelope and makes no attempt to hide his appraisal of me.

'Gina has already told us that she had some sort of breakdown when she was a child,' he says, after a moment. 'Is that what the records are about? We've searched the NHS database and couldn't find any history for her at all apart from the usual childhood ailments.'

I pull the envelope back towards me and rip it open and take out the thick wad of papers. If he's not going to bother, I'll have to do it for him. 'It's all documented there. We took her to see a private psychiatrist, so maybe that's why you don't have the records.'

'I see,' Doctor Harper says, nodding his head. I don't think he sees at all. I have the feeling that I'm being judged and found wanting; or perhaps everyone who visits a secure psychiatric hospital feels that way.

We were absolutely desperate about Georgina's behaviour and the family GP wasn't in the slightest bit interested when we took her to see him. He was completely useless and said he'd put her on the waiting list to see a counsellor if we thought it was really necessary. He didn't think there was a problem. Georgina didn't help matters; she behaved impeccably whilst we were in the GP's room, of course, giving no indication of the absolute hell that she'd put us through. The idiotic GP looked at Donald and I as if we were neurotic parents who were imagining things.

I push the wad of papers across the desk to Doctor Harper but he still makes no move to pick them up.

'I'll look at those later,' he says, glancing down at them. 'But it would be more useful if you could tell me in your own words about Gina.'

'It started when she was twelve,' I say, with a sigh. 'Puberty,' I add, as if that explains everything. I'm being forced to relieve the stress all over again and I wonder what on earth possessed me to come here. Donald says it's guilt. Although I have no idea what I'm supposed to feel guilty about because none of it was my fault. I did my best. Which is more than I can say for him; maybe he's feeling guilty and that's the real reason he won't come. I tried to persuade him but he point blank refused and said *he'd washed his hands of the girl* a long time ago and had no intention of dragging *all that business up* again. It's also a fact that there's no mental illness at all in my family whereas his mother always was neurotic. Not that he'll admit it.

'Mrs Richardson,' Doctor Harper prompts.

'We had new neighbours move in next door to us,' I state. 'And their daughter was Lissa.' Dr Harper widens his eyes in surprise and I pause for a moment before continuing. 'Georgina and Lissa became friends and spent the summer holidays going about together like girls do. Georgina was very happy and everything seemed fine but once they'd returned to school the friendship cooled.'

'And whose decision was that?'

'Lissa's,' I say. 'Although Georgina never told us they were no longer friends; she continued to call at Lissa's home every morning even though Lissa's mother told Georgina that Lissa had already left. Georgina refused to believe that Lissa didn't want to be her friend and began, well, stalking her, I suppose.'

'In what way was she stalking her?' asks Doctor Harper. 'She *was* only twelve.'

'She was, but you don't know what Georgina is like. She lives in a different world from the rest of us and will simply not be told anything. Lissa's mother told me that Georgina stuck like glue to Lissa at school and wherever she was, Georgina was there, trailing after her even when Lissa completely ignored her. It was most embarrassing and I had to speak to Georgina about it but it was like water off a duck's back. She stopped calling for her and following her around at school but started watching her outside of school instead. She'd sneak out at night and hide in Lissa's back garden to try and catch a glimpse of her. We only found out by chance when we caught her sneaking back into the house in the early hours of the morning covered in leaves and mud and freezing cold. She completely blanked us as she came in and simply refused to talk about it. She got up the next morning and behaved as if nothing had happened. We watched her at night and every night was the same; she'd sit and hide in the bushes of Lissa's back garden until the sun came up and then sneak back to her room. God knows how she wasn't spotted by Lissa's parents. The ridiculous thing was that she couldn't even see Lissa because her bedroom curtains were closed.'

'And what did Gina herself have to say about it?' Doctor Harper asks.

'She behaved as if she didn't know what I was talking about. She said that her and Lissa were still the best of friends and that they'd meet outside at night to *go on adventures.* She told me that they walked to school together every day and met for lunch but it was all nonsense; all in her head. I was at my wit's end. We thought if we hid all the keys and she couldn't get out of the house, then that would put a stop to it. We locked her bedroom door but that didn't prevent her from trying; I caught her climbing out of the bedroom window. That was when we decided that she needed help because she was going to hurt herself in her desperation to get out. After visiting the GP and being told that there was a waiting list, we paid privately to see a child psychiatrist. He prescribed a course of therapy and something to help her sleep.'

Doctor Harper frowns.

'Sleeping tablets for a twelve-year-old?'

I shrug. It's not for me to question what a doctor prescribes. They stopped her midnight escapades but didn't cure her and neither did the so-called therapy.

'The psychiatrist said that Gina herself wasn't aware what she was doing; while she may have been physically hiding in Lissa's back garden, as far as she was concerned, they were out *going on adventures* that were completely real to her.

'She was having prolonged fugue states? Doctor Harper asks.

'I don't know what they were called,' I say. 'The psychiatrist explained it as blackouts; she would have hours and days even where she thought she was going about her daily life but in fact she was doing something completely different. I never quite understood it.'

Doctor Harper nods. 'Dissociative or fugue states can last for hours, weeks, even months in severe cases and seem totally real to the person affected by them. Gina's case is very complicated and not easily definable. She's very rare.'

'Anyway,' I say, to stop him from launching into a mental health lecture which I have no desire to listen to. 'We had to keep her off school because she was never where she was supposed to be and kept disappearing. The teachers were beginning to ask questions. I told the school that she'd had her appendix out and had suffered complications so would be absent for a while. She desperately wanted to go to school because she said that Lissa was missing her; she still believed that they were friends, you see. The psychiatrist told us that eventually the obsession with Lissa would wane when it wasn't reciprocated and he was right, after several weeks, it did.'

'The therapy worked?' Doctor Harper asks.

I laugh bitterly, if only it had. The doctor looks at me in surprise.

'I'm sorry,' I say, composing myself. 'It's not the slightest bit amusing. Georgina's obsession with Lissa may have been over but she'd simply transferred it onto someone else. We had an au pair living with us at the time. At first, I was pleased when they became friendly because it seemed that Georgina was being sociable and normal. She'd chat to Maria and I was relieved that she was returning to a normal state of mind. But she wasn't; she got worse, if anything, and she wouldn't leave Maria alone, the poor girl never got a minute's peace. Maria soon tired of Georgina badgering her every minute of the day so she started to ignore her and Georgina couldn't cope with it.'

'What happened?'

I shudder when I remember that day; the blood, the screaming, the absolute horror of it all.

'She tried to stab Maria. Luckily, the scissors she

used in the attempt were old and barely capable of cutting paper. She succeeded in making only surface scratches before we took them off her. Georgina said that she had to kill her because Maria and Lissa were scheming against her and she had to kill Maria to save her own life. It was all utter, garbled nonsense that made no sense at all. She was completely deranged and we had to sedate her with the sleeping tablets and lock her in her room. The au pair left that same night; we had to pay her a considerable sum of money to stop her from going to the police. The next day Georgina behaved as if none of it had happened. She asked us where Maria had gone and was oblivious to the events of the night before. She implied that we must have done something awful to Maria to make her leave.'

The doctor stares at me unsmilingly from across the desk; I know that he's blaming me but it's not my fault at all. I can't be held accountable for the behaviour of my daughter. He should be grateful that I've come here and told the truth. I could have lied or simply stayed away and saved myself the stress.

'Not going to the police is my only regret,' I continue. 'Because if those scissors had been sharp then the outcome for Maria could have been very different. We should have reported Georgina and then maybe this wouldn't have happened with Lissa now. If she'd been punished for what she'd done to Maria then maybe she would have thought twice about trying to kill Lissa.'

'Gina is mentally ill,' Doctor Harper says. 'A person with mental illness cannot be responsible for their actions.'

I say nothing; he can say what he likes, *I* know differently. Georgina may be ill but she most certainly knows what she's doing.

'Gina tells us that you were cruel to her,' Doctor Harper says, as he realises that I'm not going to answer him.

'That doesn't surprise me,' I say. 'She always blames everyone else for her failings. We tried everything to help her, spared no expense on endless sessions with the psychiatrist. And she *did* eventually recover. She was able to go back to school after Christmas and continue her studies. We gave that girl everything.'

'You misunderstand me, I'm not saying I agree with her,' Doctor Harper says, with a sad smile. 'I'm just telling you Gina's perspective.'

'I'll leave you with the records,' I say, terminating the conversation. I stand up. I've no desire to sit here and be interrogated and made to feel at fault any longer. 'Maybe they'll help with her treatment.'

'Thank you.' Doctor Harper stands up and walks towards the door.

'Can I ask.' He pulls the door open. 'Is there anything that you'd like me to tell Gina? Is there a message I can give her?'

I think about his question for a moment before

replying.

'No,' I say, as I walk out through the doorway. 'No message.'

CHAPTER TWENTY-ONE

Gina

As I walk into the room and see who's sitting there, I feel immense disappointment but try my best to hide it.

'Hello, Gina.' Trudy beams at me.

'Hi, Trudy,' I say.

'Where's Doctor Harper?' I ask.

'Doctor Harper is a bit busy at the moment so I'm afraid you'll have to make do with me.' Doctor Wilson pulls a rueful face and laughs her hiccupy laugh and I manage to stretch my lips into the semblance of a smile.

'He may join us later if he's able but please, make yourself comfy and we'll make a start.' She indicates the armchair opposite her and I sit down and settle myself into it. Doctor Wilson, or Trudy, as she insists all the patients call her, is very nice. My appointments have been shared between Trudy and Doctor Harper. Alistair.

I don't like change, especially when it involves my psychiatrist. I never realised this until after several sessions with Alistair; we talked about my outlook on life and I gradually came to realise that I'm a person who likes routine and for things to stay the same. I don't cope very well with change. This is one of the reasons why Lissa so upset me; I was used to living on my own and having another person in the house upset my equilibrium. Had I known this I would never have advertised for a lodger and all of this mess could have been avoided.

Alistair and Trudy maintain that Lissa wasn't the only trigger for what happened because I was already unravelling before she arrived. They insist that I was extremely vulnerable because I'd moved house and taken on a huge mortgage. They say that I would have already been struggling to cope and the move was the reason I let things slide at work. Even now I have no memories of what happened with my business because in my mind I was going to work, seeing clients and conducting my business as I always had. Alistair says that when I thought I was at work I was imagining living the other life that I'd imagined for myself with James.

I agreed with them about the house move being the trigger, because what else could I do? I've learned from my fellow inmates in the months that I've been here that it's best to agree with the psychiatrist's diagnosis if you ever want to get out. I nod and agree and confirm what they say but I know that the house move had nothing to do with what happened.

It was all down to Lissa.

And James, too, because I think that maybe I spent too much time seeing him when I should have been concentrating on work. I fell head over heels in love and I put him above everything, even my business.

Not that it matters now; that's all in the past and I have to look to the future.

'So, Gina, how have you been since your last session with Doctor Harper?' Trudy asks.

I find it strange how the doctors insist that we call them by their first names but if they refer to each other it's always by their full title.

'Very well,' I say, with a smile. 'I've been continuing the daily yoga and meditation exercises and also, I've starting the painting therapy class and I love it. I'm feeling much calmer now.'

'Good, good.' She looks down at my file and reads the notes that Alistair made on Tuesday. I wish Alistair was here; he gave me no idea that he wouldn't be. Although I have to be careful and not let Trudy know that I'm thinking this. I have a sudden fear that *they've* found out but manage to control my fear; there's no way that they could know.

'You have settled down in your time with us, you've taken to the therapy extremely well and the staff and clients on the unit all speak very well of you.'

She beams at me as if this should please me but all I feel is irritation – although I hide my feelings with a sickening smile of my own. It's humiliating enough that reports of my behaviour are elicited from the staff but as to asking the other *clients* their opinion of me; that really is beyond belief. They're not *clients,* they're inmates, and most of them haven't got a hope in hell of ever getting out of here because they're all completely round the bend.

Do they think that by calling us *clients* it's going to make every one of us forget that we're in here because we've been sectioned and have absolutely *no* choice about it? It's laughable. But I daren't even laugh at an inappropriate moment because I'm being watched the *entire* time. A laugh, a frown, a flash of temper, a day where I can't be bothered to wash my hair or wear fresh clothes; it's all recorded and analysed in excruciating detail. If a random selection of people were pulled off the street and put in here, they'd be hard pushed to ever get themselves released. This place is enough to drive you properly mad with the constant questioning and watching.

'I've made some good friends on the unit,' I lie. 'And now I'm much calmer I'm so shocked at the series of events that brought me here. I'm not sure how I'm ever going to be able to forgive myself for the way I behaved.'

I say pretty much the same thing in different ways at each session; it's what they like to hear and what is required to get me out of here. This is where talking to the other *clients* has been useful; quite a few of them have been in and out like yo-yos so they know the drill for what the psychiatrists want to hear.

We've been through all the childhood stuff, over and over again, and I've pretty much blamed my parents – especially my mother – as that seems to be expected. It also suits me because besides Lissa, she is the one at fault.

'I understand your mother came to visit but you refused to see her?' Trudy asks.

I knew this would be one of their questions and I knew I'd have to be careful how I replied. It's not acceptable to say you hate your parents, even if you do. You can moan about them and blame them but not hate them; hatred is not allowed.

'Yes, I did. I gave a lot of thought as to whether I should see her but came to the conclusion that some relationships are best ended.' I smile, sadly, before adding. 'For both our sakes.'

Trudy scribbles in her notebook and I don't know whether that was a good answer or not. I couldn't tell her the truth; besides never wanting to see my mother again I knew that if I did, she would use whatever I said to her against me to make sure they never released me. No doubt she told them a pack of lies anyway but I'm certainly not going to help her.

'Now Gina, on your last session with Doctor Harper you discussed what will happen when you leave here. Have you thought any more about this? I see that you told Doctor Harper that you didn't think you were ready.'

I frown and stay silent for a moment as if I'm thinking about what I'm going to say even though I already have my answer prepared.

'I think,' I say, eventually. 'That I'm not quite ready yet but I will be soon. I think I need to stay here a little longer just to make sure that I have all my coping strategies in place.' I know this is what they want to hear because lots of the others have told me. Say yes, I want to leave immediately and the doctors will be suspicious of me and wonder whether I'm really better or just pretending so I can get out of here. Equally, if I say that I'm not sure when I might be ready, they may judge that I'm a long way from recovery and I could be stuck here forever.

Trudy smiles reassuringly and scribbles in her notebook. Of course I want to leave; I'd leave this very minute if I could but I have to be careful. Although I've been told that the CPS are unlikely to press charges, if I appear to have recovered from my mental illness too quickly, they might possibly change their minds. Especially if Lissa is whining in their ear, which I'm sure she is. Although I don't see why I should be charged because it's not as if I murdered anyone; Lissa suffered a few cuts and bruises but it was only what she deserved for stealing James away from me. Maybe she'll behave herself in future and keep her knickers on.

'And how do you feel about James and Lissa now?' Trudy asks, as if she's read my mind.

I brush my hair back with my hand and sigh.

'I feel *so* bad,' I lie. 'Lissa was such a good friend to me and I'll never forgive myself for treating her the way I did or for causing the accident. I don't expect her to forgive me – and why should she – but I'm going to write to her and apologise anyway.'

'And James?' Trudy prompts.

'I feel embarrassed,' I say, with a rueful smile. 'How could I have fabricated a relationship with someone that I'd met only once? It hardly seems believable to me now and I feel so bad about it.'

'Don't feel bad about it,' Trudy says, soothingly. 'You were in the midst of a severe and prolonged episode and the relationship was very real to you even though it didn't exist.'

I nod, as if I agree with her.

Of course, I don't agree at all. I'm simply telling her what she wants to hear. The relationship between James and I was very real and it was the intervention of that trollop, Lissa, that ruined it. I will never forgive Lissa and as for James; we're over. I'm a forgiving person but his behaviour has shown him in a new light and he's not the man I thought he was. I can do far better for myself than James and I deserve someone who will love and cherish me – not cheat on me with the first floozy who throws herself at him. Any feelings that I had for him are dead and I'm never going to undervalue myself again.

'Doctor Harper and I have been discussing your case and we think that you'd benefit from a few more weeks here before you go home but that some days out from the unit before that would be beneficial. How do you feel about that?'

'I think that would be a good thing,' I say.

'Excellent.' A tap on the door interrupts us, the door opens and Alistair enters.

'Hi, Gina. He nods at me and then Trudy. 'Doctor Wilson.' He pulls a chair next to Trudy's and sits down, stretching his long legs out in front of him.

I smile and mutter *hello* and try not to show my delight. We have to be so careful that no one discovers our relationship; one hint that we're in love and that'll be the end of our sessions and the end of Alistair's career.

'Gina and I were just discussing her reintegration into life outside the hospital, weren't we, Gina?' Trudy says.

'We were,' I agree. 'I think that some days out to get used to life outside are a very good idea.'

'Excellent.' Alistair steeples his fingers together and rests them underneath his chin. 'To start with you'll be accompanied by someone from the unit but once you're comfortable with everything you can go out alone.' His eyes twinkle and I struggle to stop myself from leaping up and flinging my arms around him. If only he were able to take me on one of the days out; sadly, he's far too valuable so it'll be left to one of the nurses.

We have to be *so* careful that no one finds out about us. Although Alistair has never actually *said* the words *I love you,* there's no doubting that he does from the way he looks at me. We have our own secret code for telling each other our feelings without anyone else knowing. A look here, a tip of the head, the steepling of his fingers – that's code for *I love you* and he does it *all* the time. When I think back to how I felt about James it was nothing compared to this. I *properly* love Alistair; I can even overlook the fact that his diagnosis of my illness is flawed because no one is completely perfect.

This is real love.

'I think I'm ready,' I say, with a smile. 'And I'm looking forward to it.'

'Excellent,' Alistair says, giving me his secret smile that tells me that we'll soon be together. I feel so happy and so lucky that I've found him. The moment I met him I knew that fate had brought us together.

He's the one I've been waiting for.

CHAPTER TWENTY-TWO

Lissa

I look through the window onto the street below and watch as the burly looking men unlock the doors of the removal lorry. I wonder how they're going to feel when they realise that the lift is small and if they have anything bigger than an armchair to bring in, they'll be humping it up the stairs. Luckily for them it'll only be up one flight as the flat next door is the only vacant one in this block. Looks like I'm going to have a new neighbour at last.

I step back from the window and kneel back down on the floor next to the Christmas tree that I've bought, to resume decorating it. It's smallish; only just over four-feet tall, not like the seven-foot monsters that Hugh and I used to have. It's probably too big for this room but I don't care; I want the place to look Christmassy and like a proper home.

It's over eight months since Hugh and I divorced and my third month of living in this apartment and oddly enough, I'm enjoying living here on my own. Hugh and I never speak now and were barely on speaking terms during our divorce proceedings. He turned into a complete arsehole and once his new bint had got her feet under the table, I was bombarded with solicitor's letters to make sure that every penny possible was shaved off my share of the proceeds from the house. Hugh carried through on his threat to make me pay my own debts off so I received far less than he did.

I cringe now when I remember how I asked him to get back with me. What possessed me? To think that I was even contemplating having a baby to please him; it's absolutely incomprehensible to me now. Thank God he turned me down otherwise I'd be surrounded by baby vomit and shit and living a life of weeping nipples with a ruined body. The mere thought of it makes me shudder.

When the finances were finally sorted I had enough to buy a two-bedroom apartment outright or get a mortgage and buy a house. I plumped for an apartment because if I had a house, it would have a garden and I'd have to look after it and I never did a thing in the garden when Hugh and I were together, Hugh did it all. The only thing I did was to sunbathe in it when the weather was decent. I never even had a washing line; everything went into the tumble dryer or to the dry cleaners. We had occasional barbeques in the summer but quite honestly, was I going to bother? No, I was not, because Hugh always did the barbeques and I don't even like barbequed food that much because it always tastes burnt to me. Well, Hugh's did, anyway. No, I didn't need a garden because it would just be one more thing to worry about.

Not that I worry.

Well, not much, anyway.

I bought a flat and it's paid for so I don't need to pay a mortgage every month and apart from my bills I have plenty of spare cash to do with as I like. I thought that I'd carry on as I had before – beauty treatments, Botox, spa days, designer clothes, all the stuff that I used to buy, but I haven't.

Honestly, I have so many clothes that I don't need any more; some of the ones I have haven't even been worn and still have the price tags hanging from them. I still like beauty treatments but I tend to buy the lotions and potions and do it in the privacy of my own bathroom now. As for Botox, well, I don't actually *need* it so why bother?

My face has healed remarkably well, and much better than most people, the doctors tell me. And with a layer of makeup you'd never know the scars were there and even without makeup they're not really noticeable, just very faint lines. But my face is no longer perfect, my skin is no longer completely unblemished and more importantly, I don't feel quite the same. I don't want beauticians slapping stuff on my face and scrutinising the scars, or, God forbid, asking me about them.

I still hate Gina for what she did to me but I'm having counselling to try and get past it because I don't want to become all bitter and twisted. I do wish Gina dead, and that's a fact, and I can't imagine that ever changing. Sometimes I even fantasise about killing her but I'm trying to stop doing that because it's not healthy. Although it's not as if I'd actually do it, so really, where's the harm?

Not that I've told the counsellor any of this and I'm not sure if I ever will because some things are best left unsaid.

I'd feel better if she'd gone to prison or got some sort of punishment but she got away with it; completely got away with it. What Gina did to me was barely even reported in the news because she's got *mental health issues* and the media are scared to death to report anything about anyone who's gone bat-shit crazy. So somehow, although I'm the totally innocent one in all of this, I'm the one who's suffered and she's got a get out of jail free card for being mental.

The only good thing to come out of it all is that I haven't heard a peep from Simon since the day of the accident, not so much as a text, threatening or otherwise. I'm guessing that the police turning up at his door to question him about Gina put the fear of the God into him. This is a massive relief as I was a bit afraid of him. He's no longer my client, in fact he's no longer a client of the agency so perhaps he feels a bit embarrassed about it. I sometimes wonder if the way he treated me might have something to do with my pathetic attempt to get Hugh back.

I haven't so many men friends now as I used to have.

Well, actually, I haven't any at the moment and I'm rather enjoying being on my own.

After I came out of hospital and stayed at Mum and Dad's I obviously didn't see anyone then because I had two arms in plaster. And it was funny, because even when the plaster came off and my face had healed and I returned to work, I still stayed with them. I thought I'd be itching to move out to get away from the nagging and smothering but I wasn't. The nagging was nowhere near as bad as I thought it would be and it was quite nice to be looked after. I couldn't have my men friends stay over and I couldn't stay over at theirs, because it would have required too much explaining but I found that I didn't care; it was quite nice to have a break from men. I ended up staying at Mum and Dad's until I moved here three months ago.

I've found out who my real friends are too; because real friends stick around during the bad times, don't they? I discovered that from my vast circle of friends, only a few have stuck around and they're not the ones I thought they'd be. The friends that I used to go out partying with were the first to go because obviously I was in no fit state to socialise. They were swiftly followed by the clients that had become friends. Once I was no longer visiting them on a regular basis, they stopped calling me so they weren't really friends at all, were they?

I can now count on one hand the number of people that I consider a friend but that's okay, because I only have so much time to see people so I don't need to spread myself so thin. Rachel, one of the other interior designers that I work with is now one of my best friends. We'd always got on but I never really got to know her until I returned to work after the accident. I was struggling a bit. She stepped in without me needing to ask and basically helped me get back on my feet.

She's coming over soon. We're going to have some lunch and then walk into town and do some Christmas shopping; one of the benefits of my new home is that it's only a ten-minute walk from the town centre.

Rachel is forty and divorced, like me, and she's happily single and has no intention of ever settling down again. She says no way is she putting up with a man again as she likes to please herself and do what she wants. Maybe she has a point; the jury is still out on that one for me.

I hang the last bauble on the tree then stand up and place the chunky, silver star on the very top. It looks a bit precarious but hopefully it'll hold.

I go out into the kitchen and quickly put the quiche onto a plate and tip the salad out of the bag and into a bowl. I take them into the lounge and place them both on the table. I've already set it with two plates, cutlery and two small wine glasses. I have a bottle of Prosecco chilling in the fridge but I'll have to be strict and make sure we only have one glass each otherwise the shopping trip will get forgotten.

I've just finished when the doorbell rings. That'll be Rachel, she always arrives dead on time, unlike me. I give the tiny table in the corner of the lounge one more glance to ensure it looks nice and head down the hallway to the front door.

I open the front door to Rachel; she's wearing a fake-fur coat over black trousers with towering stiletto heels. Her brunette hair is piled in a glossy up-do and as usual, she looks impossibly glamorous.

'Hi! I hope you're ready for some serious shopping,' she says, as she air kisses each side of my head.

'You bet,' I reply. 'Just as soon as we've had lunch. We need sustenance.' I step aside to let her in but she pauses at the sound of the lift doors opening.

'Hey,' she says, pointing her head towards the left. 'It's your new neighbour.'

'What?'

'Getting out of the lift,' she says, quietly. 'I saw her downstairs ordering the removal men around.

Let's introduce ourselves and find out a bit about her.'

I can't help feeling relieved that it's a woman and not a man. For some odd reason I had a feeling that a creepy womaniser was going to move in and I wouldn't be able to shake him off. Although I have no idea why I thought that because the guy who lived there before never spoke so much as a word to me. He was a bit nerdy looking and always looked at the floor on the rare occasion that we met in the corridor.

'God, you're so nosey,' I say, with a giggle. I can't see the lift from my doorway so have no idea whether the woman is young or old.

'What?' She laughs and affects to be offended. 'I'm simply looking out for a mate. I have to make sure that the person living next door is suitable.'

'Okay, but let's not stand chatting for ages,' I say, quietly. 'I want to get to the shops before they close.' Rachel is a notorious talker, even worse than me, and if we're not careful she'll end up inviting the new neighbour in and we'll spend the afternoon getting to know her and our planned shopping trip will be forgotten.

Rachel laughs. 'Cheeky bitch,' she says, as she winks at me.

The clip clop of heels gets closer and Rachel puts on her best smile.

'Hi! I guess you're moving into number nine? I'm Rachel and this here is Lissa.'

'Nice to meet you,' I say, as I step out into the

hallway, eager to meet my closest neighbour. 'I'm Lissa.'

The smile slides from my face and I stare at my new neighbour in disbelief.

No, it can't be.

'Hello,' Gina says to Rachel, before turning to me. 'And hello, I'm Georgina, so nice to meet you both.'

I gawp at her, unable to believe it's her and she beams a smile at both of us.

Oh God, here we go again......

THE END

Thank you so much for reading this book, I really do appreciate it. I do hope that you've enjoyed it and if you have, I'd be thrilled if you took the time to leave a review or star rating on Amazon/and or Goodreads.